# ONLY
# LOVE

# ONLY LOVE

*Erich Segal*

G. P. PUTNAM'S SONS / NEW YORK

G. P. PUTNAM'S SONS
*Publishers Since 1838*
a member of Penguin Putnam Inc.
200 Madison Avenue
New York, NY 10016

ISBN 0-399-14341-6
Printed in the United States of America
*Book design by Gretchen Achilles*

*To Karen, Francesca and Miranda,*
*my only loves*

*Le meilleur de la vie se passe à dire:*
*"Il est trop tôt," puis "Il est trop tard."*

*The better part of life is spent saying:*
*"It's too early," and then "It's too late."*

FLAUBERT
Correspondence
[July 1859 Rob. p. 543]

THIS IS A WORK OF FICTION. The Author has taken some liberties in chronology, as well as in the portrayal of certain public figures and artistic personalities. These are his own creations and not to be construed as authentic history.

Likewise, some of the scientific material has been sketched in broad strokes for the lay reader. The Author is nevertheless grateful to Doctors Jack Strominger of Harvard; Howard Fine of the Dana Farber Institute, Boston; and Rodney Rivers of St. Mary's Hospital, London, for providing factual strands to weave a fictional garment.

# ONLY
# LOVE

# PROLOGUE

I HAVE A TERRIBLE confession to make.

When I learned Silvia was dying I was not completely unhappy.

I know this may seem inhuman—especially from a doctor. But then I can't think of her as just another patient. In fact, when I first heard she was coming to see me after all this time, I almost imagined it was a gesture of reconciliation.

I wonder what's going on in her mind. Does she regard our impending reunion merely as a last desperate attempt to save her life? Or perhaps before the darkness falls, does she long to see me again as much as I long to see her?

And what about her husband? Even in the unlikely event that she hasn't told him about our relationship years ago, she would certainly have to *now*.

But whatever his feelings, he would be unable to prevent us from meeting. After all, he was a man accustomed to having the best in the world and I guess in this field I am number one.

She is two years younger than I, a mere forty-three years old. And judging even from the most recent newspaper articles, still very beautiful. She looks too radiant, too *alive* to be seriously ill. To me, she has always been the quintessence of the life force.

In our first telephone conversation, Rinaldi is polite and formal. Though speaking of his wife, there is no trace of emotion in his voice. On the contrary, he takes for granted that I will be instantly at his disposal.

"Mrs. Rinaldi has a brain tumor—can you see her right away?"

Yet for all his arrogance I can sense an implicit acknowledgment that I have a power he himself does not possess. Consummate businessman that he is, he still cannot outbargain the Angel of Death.

And that is a source of satisfaction.

Yet suddenly, almost as an afterthought, he adds with a barely perceptible break in his voice, "Please."

I had to help. Both of them.


THE NOTES AND X-RAYS reached my office within the hour. As soon as I was alone I tore open the envelope, thinking, irrationally, that there might be something recognizably Silvia inside.

But of course these were only various high-tech images of her brain. Ironically, I thought I had seen inside her before. But the mind is not an organ. The brain is not the seat of the soul. And then the physician in me grew angry.

Even the earliest scans showed evidence of neoplasm. What kind of people had she consulted? I leafed quickly through the notes but it was the usual antiseptic medical jargon. The patient, a then forty-one-year-old married white female, first came to one Professor Luca Vingiano, complaining of severe headaches. He attributed the cause to emotional stress and prescribed state-of-the-art tranquilizers.

But then despite his *far niente* philosophy, he had let slip a bit of personal detail. Evidently there was some unspecified tension in Silvia's life. Perhaps self-servingly, I immediately assumed that it involved her marriage.

For though she appeared with her husband in photos as a kind of marital ornament, she always seemed deliberately to exist on the margin of his life. Nico, by contrast, was a far more public person. In addition to being Italy's largest car manufacturer, FAMA (Fabbrica Milanese Automobili), his multinational colossus, included construction, steel works, insurance and publishing.

At various times there had been rumors in the press linking him with one or another talented younger woman. Of course the photographs they shot were all at charity occasions, so this may have been mere scabrous speculation. But then eminence always attracts gossip. I myself had achieved enough success in my field to know that.

Whatever the reality, the suggestion was like a lit match for the dry tinderwood of my emotions. And I chose to believe the journalistic innuendos, and ascribed the anxiety noted by the good professor to her husband's alienated affections.

I forced myself to read on.

She had languished for an unconscionably long time before Vingiano took her seriously and sent her to a London neurologist with a "Sir" before his name and an international reputation behind it.

He found the tumor all right but adjudged it to be now inoperable. Indeed, there was no way that the most skilled pair of hands could maneuver the tiniest microsurgical instrument and not cause serious damage. Or more likely kill her.

This made me the last resort. And it was an uncomfortable feeling. True enough, the genetic technique I pioneered had several times succeeded in reversing tumor growth by replicating the DNA, correcting the problem, and then reinfusing it to the patient.

Yet now, for the first time, I fully understood why doctors are not meant to treat people close to them. I was suddenly insecure and lost faith in my abilities. Dealing with someone you care for makes you painfully aware of your own fallibility.

I did not want Silvia as a patient.

SCARCELY FIFTEEN MINUTES after the envelope had reached my hand, the phone rang.

"Well, Dr. Hiller, what do you think?"

"I'm sorry, I haven't had time to go through the whole history."

"Wouldn't a quick glance at her latest scans tell you everything you need to know?"

Obviously he was right. And I wondered if he didn't want to prevent me from reading too much detail in the records. Did he fear I would blame him for not acting more swiftly? (In a way I did.)

"Mr. Rinaldi, I'm afraid I agree with your doctor in London. This kind of growth is incurable."

"Except by you," he countered insistently. I guess I was waiting for him to say it. "Can you see her today?"

Reflexively, I glanced in my diary. My afternoon was packed and I had a seminar at 4:30 P.M. Why had I even looked when I knew I would accede to his demands? (To be frank, I was relieved at how swiftly it would occur. There was now no chance of me spending a sleepless night in anticipation.)

"How about two?" I proposed.

But I had miscalculated Nico's capacity for gratitude. I should have guessed he would try for a better deal.

"Actually, our apartment is only a few minutes away. We can be there almost immediately."

"All right," I surrendered with a sigh. Let's get it over with.

MINUTES LATER MY SECRETARY buzzed to announce the arrival of Mr. and Mrs. Niccolo Rinaldi.

My heart began to race. Within seconds my office doors would open—and with them a torrent of memories. I would not breathe again until I caught sight of her.

I SAW HIM FIRST: tall, imposing and intense. Receding forehead. He acknowledged me with a saturnine nod, and presented his wife as if introducing her for the first time.

I stared at Silvia's face. At first it seemed unchanged by time. Her eyes were the same black flames, though they were deliberately avoiding mine. I could not decipher her emotions, but I gradually became aware that something was different.

Perhaps it was my imagination, but there seemed to be a weariness and nonspecific sadness unrelated to her illness. To my mind, it was the expression of a life lived on the far side of happiness.

As I moved forward awkwardly (or so it seemed) to shake her husband's hand, I said quietly to Silvia:

"It's good to see you again."

PART ONE

# SPRING
# 1978

# ONE

THE RENDEZVOUS was Paris. Those of us who survived the initial third degree and the rigorous training that followed would be rewarded by being sent to Africa to risk our lives and hopefully save others. It was my first trip east of Chicago.

Our flight arrived just as day was breaking. Ten thousand feet below, the city was stirring, a sensuous woman shaking off the languor of sleep in the early morning light.

An hour later, having checked my stuff at the Aérogare, I bounded up the steps from the Métro into the very center of St. Germain des Prés, which pulsated with the *musique concrète* of the rush-hour traffic.

I glanced nervously at my watch—only fifteen minutes to go. I checked my street map for the final time and then sprinted like mad all the way to the

Headquarters of Médecine Internationale, a sclerotic architectural antique on the rue des Saints Pères.

I arrived sweaty but under the wire.

"Sit down, Dr. Hiller."

François Pelletier, the irascible grand inquisitor, was a dead ringer for Don Quixote, including the wispy beard. The only difference was his shirt, open nearly to the navel. And the cigarette dangling from his bony fingers.

Appropriately enough, he was flanked by a balding Sancho Panza type, who scribbled compulsively on a pad, and a well-upholstered Dutch woman in her early thirties (Dulcinea?).

From the moment the interview began, it was obvious that François had a chip on his shoulder about Americans. He held them collectively responsible for all the ills of mankind from nuclear waste to high cholesterol.

He bombarded me with hostile questions, to which at first I responded politely and professionally. But when it became clear there was no end in sight, I began to retort sarcastically, wondering when the next flight back to Chicago left.

After nearly an hour he was still grilling me about every microscopic aspect of my life. For example: why did I not burn my draft card during the Vietnam War?

I answered by asking if he had burned *his* when the French were fighting there before us.

He quickly changed the subject and we continued volleying unpleasantries.

"Tell me, Dr. Hiller, do you know where Ethiopia is?"

"Don't insult my intelligence, Dr. Pelletier."

"What if I told you that three other Americans I interviewed thought it was in South America?"

"Then I'd tell you they were assholes. And you shouldn't bother with them."

"Right on both counts." He now jumped to his feet and began to pace. Then suddenly stopped, whirled and fired.

"Imagine for a moment you are in a run-down field hospital, in the wilds of Africa, miles from everything you ever knew as civilization. How would you keep your sanity?"

"Bach," I answered, unblinking.

"What?"

"Johann Sebastian—or any of his relatives, for that matter. I always start my day with fifty push-ups, fifty sit-ups and two or three bracing partitas and fugues."

"Ah yes. From your CV I gather you're quite a musician. Unfortunately our clinics don't include pianos."

"That's okay. I can play in my head and get the same buzz. I've got this portable keyboard that I can take with me. It doesn't make any noise. It'll keep my fingers nimble while the music keeps my soul in shape."

For the first time that morning I seemed to have short-circuited the electric current of antagonism. What possible rock could he throw at me now? My mind was in a high state of alertness.

"Well," he mused, eyeing me up and down. "You haven't cracked up yet."

"You sound disappointed."

François fixed me with his gaze then queried, "How about filth? Starvation? And appalling diseases?"

"I've done my year in the Pits. I think I can take every conceivable medical horror show."

"Leprosy? Smallpox?"

"No, I admit I've never seen an actual case of either in the state of Michigan. Are you trying to turn me off?"

"In a way," he conceded, leaning conspiratorially closer and sending some particularly foul smoke in my direction. "Because if you're going to freak out, it's a lot better to do it here than in the middle of Africa."

Now the Dutch woman suddenly decided to put her two cents in.

"Tell me, why would you want to go to the Third World when you could be making house calls on Park Avenue?"

"How does wanting to help people grab you?"

"Fairly predictable," Sancho commented as he took it down. "Can't you come up with anything more original?"

I was rapidly losing my patience—and my temper.

"Frankly, you guys disappoint me. I thought Médecine Internationale was full of altruistic doctors, not pain-in-the-ass cynics."

The three interrogators looked at one another and then François turned to me and asked bluntly, "Now, what about sex?"

"Not here, François. Not in front of everybody," I retorted. By this time I didn't give a shit.

His minions broke into laughter and he did too. "That also answers my most important question, Matthew. You have a sense of humor." He reached out his hand. "Welcome aboard."

By this point I wasn't sure I wanted to be on board. But then I had journeyed so far and gone through such crap that I thought I would take their offer and at least sleep on it.

The three-week orientation course for Eritrea would begin the day after next. So I had forty-eight hours to see the glories of Paris.

I CHECKED INTO THE LEFT BANK DUMP they had reserved for the candidates and decided it had atmosphere. It was one of those fleabags in which every room, I'm sure, was a garret and every bedspring creaked. Maybe François chose it to toughen us for the trip.

My brother, Chaz, had told me that it was impossible to get a bad meal in Paris. And he was absolutely right. I ate in a place called Le Petit Zinc, where you picked your meal from all sorts of exotic crustaceans displayed downstairs, which they then served on the upper floors. If I had had the guts to ask the names of the things I was eating, I probably wouldn't have enjoyed them as much.

THE NEXT TWO DAYS were a shock to my system. Trying to see the artistic treasures of Paris in so short a time is like trying to swallow an elephant in one gulp. But I gave it my best. From dawn till well after dusk, I absorbed the city through every pore.

After they kicked me out of the Louvre and locked the doors, I grabbed a quick dinner at a nearby bistro. I wandered along the Boulevard St. Michel until I was too exhausted to go anywhere but up to join the cockroach party in my room.

As I sat down for what seemed like the first time all day, the jet lag that had been chasing me since I arrived finally caught me with a flying tackle.

I barely had time to take off my shoes and fall back onto the bed, lapsing into a post-Parisian coma.

———

OF COURSE I REMEMBER the exact date: Monday, April 3, 1978. Yet it started like any other morning: I shaved and showered, selected my coolest shirt (blue button-down, short-sleeved) and then headed for the rue des Saints Pères and Operation Eritrea, Day One.

By now I had recovered my confidence and sharpened my ideals and was ready for anything.

Except the emotional ambush awaiting me.


MOST OF THE OTHERS were already there, chattering over paper cups of coffee. Between puffs, François introduced me to four French candidates (one a fairly attractive female), two Dutchmen, one wearing a ten-gallon hat who would be doing most of the anesthesia (don't ask me the connection).

And Silvia.

I stopped breathing. She was a poem without words.

Everything about her was exquisite. She had the face of a Medusa in reverse. One glance turned you into jelly.

She wore jeans, sweatshirt and no makeup. Her long black hair was pulled back in a ponytail. But this didn't fool anyone.

"Don't hold Silvia's looks against her, Matthew. She's such an astute diagnostician that I picked her even though her grandfather was a fascist and her father causes lung cancer."

"Hi," I managed though in oxygen-debt. "I can understand the sins of the grandfather, but what would make her dad carcinogenic?"

"Simple," François grinned. "His last name is Dalessandro."

"You mean head of FAMA—the Italian carmakers?"

"The very same. Arch-polluters of the highways and byways. Not to mention the chemical waste they produce. . . ." François seemed to convey this information with a kind of perverse glee.

I looked at her and asked, "Is he pulling my leg again?"

"No—guilty as charged," she allowed. "But notice that the latter-day St. Luke forgot to mention that my ecologically delinquent *father* fought with the *American* army during the war. Where are you from, Matthew?"

"By coincidence, another automotive capital: Dearborn, Michigan. Only my name's not Ford."

"Lucky you. Coming from a well-known and, in my case, notorious family can sometimes be a drag."

Pointing to me, François confided mischievously to her, "By the way, Silvia, watch out for this character. He tries to come across as a simple shit-kicker from the cornfields. But he's a serious pianist, and speaks Italian."

"Really?" she looked at me, sort of impressed.

"It's nowhere near as fluent as your English. But you really need the language when you major in music."

"Ah, *un amante dell'opera?*" she asked eagerly.

"Yes. You too?"

"Madly. But when you're born in Milan, you grow up crazy about two things: football and opera—*la scalciata* and *La Scala.*"

"And *la scaloppina,*" I added, proud of my alliteration.

At this moment François bellowed, "Now everybody sit down and shut up. The cocktail hour's over."

Suddenly the banter ceased and the thoughts of those present focused on healing. We each grabbed a seat (Silvia and two others sat cross-legged on the floor).

"Let me make a prediction," François revved up. "Whoever doesn't already dislike me will absolutely hate my guts by the end of the first week in the field. It's going to be hot, stressful and dangerous. The conditions you'll encounter are like nothing you've ever known. Before this civil war, Ethiopia was already one of the poorest countries in the world—per capita income ninety dollars a year. The people live in a perpetual state of starvation exacerbated by endless years of drought. It's a full-fledged nightmare."

He took a breath and then said, "Now, appropriately enough, we'll start with the plague."

Project #62 of Médecine Internationale was under way.

I THINK WHEN IT COMES TO WOMEN, I have a Groucho Marx complex. The minute they express interest in me, I begin to scamper in the opposite direction. Thus it was that morning in Paris.

Not Silvia, of course, but with Denise Lagarde.

She was a pert, quick-witted internist from Grenoble with, as the French put it so picturesquely, "a well-stacked balcony" (it's amazing how quickly you pick up important vocabulary). In any other context, she would have looked extremely appetizing.

For dinner, we all went to a restaurant which, believe it or not, served more than two hundred different kinds of cheeses. Under ordinary circumstances I would have been in culinary heaven. But my taste buds, like my other sensory organs, were numb. The initial impact of Silvia was that profound.

Denise contrived to sit next to me and came on shamelessly. Three hours later, as we were drinking coffee, she murmured with unabashed candor, "I find you extremely attractive, Matthew."

I reciprocated the compliment, hoping it would not lead to where I was almost sure it would.

"Would you like me to show you Paris?"

Unfortunately I came up with a tactless answer. "Thanks, Denise. I've seen it."

She got the message and I had made my first enemy.

SILVIA WAS NEVER ALONE. She was like the Pied Piper, moving with a swarm of admirers of both sexes wherever she went.

Yet I soon realized how heavily escorted she was—in a rather sinister sense.

On that first Friday, I happened to arrive early. As I glanced casually out the window, Silvia entered my field of vision, dancing gracefully down the street and into the building. As I was savoring the view, I noticed that in addition to her usual bevy of groupies, there was a huge, barrel-chested, middle-aged guy trailing about a hundred yards behind her. I got the eerie sensation that he was stalking her. Of course, since it might have been my imagination, I said nothing.

During our half-hour lunch break (not very French, I agree) we all hung around, eating filled baguettes. Silvia went down the block to buy a newspaper. And then, moments before we were about to resume, I saw her coming back. Farther up the street, I recognized the same man, clearly watching her intently.

Now I knew it was not my imagination and was determined to alert her.

At the end of the afternoon session, when a bunch of us returned to the "Termite Hilton," as we had dubbed it, I boldly asked Silvia if she would join me for a drink and a brief chat about a private matter.

She agreed amicably enough and we repaired to a little *bistro à vin* two doors away.

"So." She smiled as I squeezed into our narrow booth, carrying a white wine in each hand. "What's happening?"

"Silvia, I'm sure you have plans for this evening. I'll make it really quick. I don't want to upset you . . ." I hesitated. "But I think there's someone following you."

"I know." She was totally unfazed.

"You do?"

"There always is. My father's worried about something happening to me."

"You mean the guy's your bodyguard?"

"Sort of. But I prefer to think of Nino as my fairy godfather. Anyway, Papa's not paranoid. I'm sorry to say there are genuine reasons. . . ." Her voice trailed off.

Oh, Jesus. Did I put my foot in it. I suddenly recalled reading about her mother's abduction and murder many years ago. It was worldwide news.

"Hey," I mumbled apologetically, "I'm sorry I asked. We can go back to the group now."

"What's the rush? Let's finish our wine and gossip for a bit. Do you follow NBA basketball?"

"Not very closely. You know when you're a resident you try to use all your free time to sleep. Why do you ask?"

"Well, FAMA has its own professional team in the European League. Every year we recruit players that get cut from the NBA. I was hoping that you'd noticed one of the Detroit Pistons who was slowing down a little but might still have a few minor-league seasons in him."

"I'll tell you what—I'll consult a specialist. When I write to my brother, Chaz, I'll ask him. He's a real sports nut."

"That's one thing I'm going to miss in Africa. Whenever the boys played in England, my father flew over and took me to watch."

"What did you do in England between games?"

"I studied there for nearly ten years after my mother died. I even did my M.D. at Cambridge."

"Ah-ha, that explains your fancy accent. What are you specializing in?"

"I haven't made up my mind. But it'll probably be something like pediatric surgery. It depends how good I am with my hands—which I'm about to find out. And you?"

"Well at first I was attracted by *lo scalpello* too. But I honestly believe that the scalpel will be obsolete in a few years and it'll all be done by various genetic techniques. That's where I'd like to end up eventually. So, after Africa, I'll probably do a Ph.D. in something like molecular biology. Anyway, I'm looking forward to this adventure, aren't you?"

"Well, just between the two of us, I sometimes wonder if I'll be able to cope."

"Don't worry. With all you had going against you, François wouldn't have picked you if he didn't think you could handle the rough stuff."

"I hope so," she murmured, still with a trace of uncertainty in her voice.

And, for the first time, I sensed that beneath that flawless exterior, there were little fireflies of doubt flashing now and then. It was nice to know that she was human.

AS WE WALKED OUT of the door, I spied Nino leaning against a parking meter, "reading" a newspaper.

"By the way, Silvia. Is he coming to Eritrea with us too?"

"No, thank God. Actually, being really on my own will be a new experience for me."

"Well, if it means anything, you can tell your father that I'll be there to protect you."

She seemed to really appreciate what I said. She smiled at me and, in so doing, destroyed all my autoimmune reactions to really falling in love with her.

# TWO

TOWARD THE END of the second week of our course, there was a once-in-a-lifetime event at the Opéra. The legendary soprano Maria Callas would be singing Violetta in *La Traviata* for the final time. This was an occasion I was determined not to miss. It was hardly mature behavior, but I faked a couple of symptoms and left the seminar early to line up for possible standing-room tickets.

Needless to say, I was not the only person in Paris and vicinity who wanted to see Callas. There seemed to be enough people ahead of me to fill every one of the two thousand–odd seats in the theater. Nevertheless, I reminded myself that I had led a clean life and if my virtue was ever to be rewarded, this would be as good a time as any.

My unspoken prayers were answered. Around six-thirty, when the queue had moved a mere twenty places and things were looking increasingly glum, I heard a female voice call out:

"Matthew, I thought you weren't feeling well?"

Caught in the act! I turned to see that it was none other than Signorina Perfect.

She had loosened her austere, workaday hairdo, letting the locks cascade onto her shoulders. She wore a simple black dress, which revealed considerably more leg than her usual jeans. In short, she was stunning.

"I'm okay," I explained, "but I just had to see Callas. Anyway, I'm being punished for playing hooky because it doesn't look like I'm going to make it."

"Well, then join me. My father's company has a box here and I'm on my own tonight."

"I'd love to. But are you sure I'm not a little overdressed for you?" I responded, indicating my frayed denim shirt and corduroy pants.

"You're not appearing on stage, Matthew. I'm the only one who'll see. Come on, we don't want to miss the overture."

She took my hand and led me past the crowd of glowering ticketless rivals, up the Great Marble Staircase into the breathtaking vaulted foyer, built with an array of red, blue, white and green marmoreal stone.

As I feared, I was the only man not wearing a dinner jacket or tails. But then, I consoled myself, I was invisible. I mean, who could notice me when at my side I had the *Venus de Milano*?

A uniformed "bellboy" led us down a hushed corridor to a wooden door which opened into a crimson velvet box. We overlooked a canyon of refined plebeians and a sky-high proscenium arch. In the center was the Opera House's fabled chandelier, hanging from a gold-circled ceiling painted by Chagall of the most famous subjects in opera and ballet (lovers seemed to predominate).

I was practically in heaven as the orchestra tuned up beneath us. We sat in the two front seats, where a half bottle of champagne awaited us. Calling upon years of experience as a waiter, I poured us each a glassful without losing a bubble. I toasted appropriately.

"To my host—" I began. "Fabbrica Milanese Automobili," adding, "and those nearest and dearest to the management."

She laughed appreciatively.

As the lights began to dim, the bearlike Nino (also in a tux) entered and sat discreetly at the back. Though he affected his usual deadpan, I wondered if he too was looking forward to the music.

"Do you know *Traviata* well?" Silvia asked.

"*Mezzo mezzo*," I replied modestly. "I wrote a paper on it in college. And yesterday after class I spent about an hour playing through the golden oldies."

"Oh, where did you find a piano?"

"I just made like I was shopping in La Voix de Son Maître, took the score down from the shelf and started tinkling on one of their Steinways. Fortunately they didn't throw me out."

"I'd love to have been there. I wish you'd told me."

"I wish I'd known. Anyway, we can go there tomorrow if you'd really like. The manager gave me an open invitation."

"That's a promise, Matthew." She raised her glass as if thanking me in advance. Her smile shone even in the darkening theater.

The opening chorus, *"Libiamo ne' lieti calici"* ("Let's drink up in happy goblets"), aptly reflected my state of mind. And even though I was intoxicated by Callas's magical stage presence, I regularly stole glances at Silvia, whose perfect profile I could study at leisure.

Half an hour later the heroine stood alone on stage and sang *"Ah fors' è lui,"* ("Perhaps *he* is the one"), recognizing that, despite her many affairs, her relationship with Alfredo was the first time in her life that she was genuinely in love.

Callas was in overdrive and with her unique powers of expression conveyed the depth of Violetta's enamorment. And, when Silvia turned to me for a second to share the moment, I dared to wonder if she herself had ever experienced this same feeling—and if so, with whom.

As the Act I curtain descended to rapturous applause, another lackey appeared with canapés and more fizz. Being a guest, I felt obliged to contribute something intellectual. I offered a rather pedantic observation.

"Do you realize that in that entire first Act there wasn't even a single break in the music, no recitative, and not even a real aria till *'Fors' è lui?'* "

"I didn't even notice."

"That's the whole trick. Verdi was diabolically clever."

"So apparently is my companion this evening."

The lights dimmed again and the tragedy began to unfold.

A few minutes later, there was a thunderous chord on the brass as Violetta realized she was doomed: "Oh Lord, to die so young." And finally Callas fainted, only to revive again long enough to sing an incredibly high B-flat—and immediately die from the effort.

The audience was so transported they were almost afraid to break the spell. Then, as the ripples of applause crescendoed into a tidal wave of adulation, I suddenly felt Silvia's hand in mine. I looked at her. She was in tears.

"I'm sorry, Matthew. I know I'm being silly." The moment was stirring, the apology gratuitous. I was feeling a bit of ocular humidity myself.

I placed my other hand on top of hers. She did not move and we remained that way until the final curtain fell.

By my count, the diva took fourteen solo bows as her worshipers rose to pay homage. I clapped for selfish reasons. As long as the verbal and floral bouquets kept flying at Callas, I would be alone with Silvia in this oasis of time.

WHEN WE FINALLY EMERGED from the theater, Nino was waiting, inconspicuously visible.

Silvia linked her arm in mine and proposed, "Shall we walk?"

"Suits me."

She made a subtle gesture to her guardian and we set off for a nocturnal promenade through the streets of Paris, passing the many brightly lit outdoor restaurants filled with theatergoers eating supper and toasting in their "happy goblets." We discussed Callas's artistry.

"You know, it's not just her voice," Silvia observed. "It's the way she breathes believable life into the character."

"Yeah, I mean especially when you consider that Verdi's original heroine weighed nearly three hundred pounds. I'm not kidding. During her death scene the audience also died—of laughter. Yet even at her age, Callas comes across as a frail young woman and not a female sumo wrestler."

A coloratura laugh of appreciation.

By the time we had walked the length of the rue St. Honoré, I offered to flag a cab—or even to hail Nino who was following us discreetly at about two miles an hour in a Peugeot (not a FAMA!). But Silvia, still overflowing with energy, insisted that we walk the rest of the way.

Just before we crossed the Seine at the Pont Neuf, we took a breather on a convenient bench. From this viewpoint the city resembled a terrestrial galaxy stretching to infinity in all directions.

As we sat there in mutual solitude, I debated with myself whether or not to share with her the tangled thoughts I was feeling. Did we know each other well enough? I wasn't sure. Yet I took a chance.

"Silvia, does *Traviata* always make you cry like that?"

She nodded. "I guess Italians are sentimental."

"So are Americans. But I've found that I relate the sadness I'm watching to events in my own life. It's a kind of socially respectable excuse to recall old griefs."

Her eyes told me that she understood completely. "You know about my mother?"

"Yes."

"You know, tonight—on the stage—when the doctor announced that Violetta was dead, I couldn't help remembering the moment when my father said those same words to me. But then I don't need an artistic pretext to mourn. I still miss her terribly."

"How has your father coped all this time?"

"Not at all, really. I mean, it's been almost fifteen years and he's still like a man under water. Occasionally we have a conversation, but most of the time he's submerged in his work. He just stays locked in his office, away from people."

"Including you?"

"I think especially me."

I wondered whether the subject was getting too difficult for her. But then she talked on willingly.

"I was only a little girl, so I could barely appreciate the things she was—the first woman editor of *La Mattina*, committed to social reform, and very brave. That's a lot to live up to. But I'd like to think she'd be pleased with what I've become—or at least trying to become."

I didn't know whether to answer with the usual pious platitudes, or say what I really believed—that dead parents survive only in their children's psyches.

She sighed and gazed out over the water. Her unhappiness was palpable.

"Hey," I said after a moment. "I'm sorry. I probably never should have brought this up in the first place."

"That's okay. There's a part of me that still needs to talk about it—about her. And the occasion of a new friend provides acceptable camouflage."

"I hope so," I said softly. "I mean I hope we'll be friends."

She reacted shyly for a moment. Then answered, "Sure. I mean, we already are."

Her tone suddenly changed. Glancing at her watch, she stood up hastily.

"Gosh, do you know what time it is? And I've still got two more articles to read for tomorrow's class."

"Which ones?"

"Typhus," she replied as we began to walk hurriedly.

"Ah," I said pontifically. "Allow me to remind you, Doctor, that there are actually three diseases subsumed under that nomenclature—"

"Yes," she offered instantly, "'epidemic,' 'Bril-Zinsser' and 'murine.'"

"That's very good," I said, perhaps inadvertently sounding patronizing.

"Come on, Matthew, you seem to have trouble believing I went to med school."

"You're right," I confessed good-humoredly. "I have a hell of a lot of trouble."

AT THE VIRTUAL DOORSTEP of day, she turned to me and smiled. "Thank you for a lovely evening."

"Hey, that was supposed to be my line."

There was an awkward pause during which conventionally we would have exchanged goodnights and parted. But instead she mentioned diffidently, "I noticed how touched you were by the opera too. Judging by the things you've said tonight, would I be right in thinking that—"

I interrupted her insight. "Yes." It was still painful to even say that much. "It was my father. I'll tell you about it sometime."

I then kissed her lightly on both cheeks and retired to the privacy of my own dreams.

# THREE

*I LOVED MY FATHER but I was ashamed of him. From as early as I can remember, he lived on an emotional seesaw. He was either "on top of the world"— or overwhelmed by it.*

*In other words, either terribly drunk or painfully sober.*

*Yet unfortunately, in either state, he was equally inaccessible to his children. I couldn't bear being in his company. There is nothing scarier for a kid than to have a parent out of control. And Henry Hiller was this in the extreme—skydiving from responsibility without a parachute.*

*He was an assistant professor of literature at Cutler Junior College in Dearborn, Michigan. I think his primary goal in life was self-destruction, and he seemed to be very good at it. He was so skillful that he even let his department find out about his drinking problem just a few months before he was to receive tenure.*

*The way he and Mom explained this career move to my little brother, Chaz, and myself was that Dad wanted to concentrate full-time on his writing. As he put it, "Lots of people just dream about producing that big book that's in all of us. But it takes real courage to take the plunge and do it without the safety net of a job."*

*My mother, on the other hand, did not call a family conference to announce that she would be taking over as both homemaker and bread-winner.*

*Since her husband was "working" late into the night, she would get up early, prepare our breakfasts and pack lunch, drive us to school, and then go to the hospital, where she had once been the head surgical nurse. But now, because of her need for flexibility, she had demoted herself to being a roving understudy for whatever department was short-handed.*

*This was a testimony to her versatility as well as her endurance. In exchange for time off in the late afternoon—to ferry us from school to various friends, dentists, and my all-important piano lessons—she had to return and work several hours in the evenings. Unfortunately this did not count as overtime.*

*While she was taking care of all of us, who the hell was taking care of her? She was perpetually tired, with bottomless rings around her eyes.*

*I tried to grow up as fast as possible to assume my share of the burden. At first Chaz was too young to understand what was going on. And I did what I could to protect his innocence. Which really boiled down to minimizing his contact with Dad.*

WHEN I WAS TEN I *proposed to my mother that, to ease some of the pressure on her, I leave school and seek employment. She laughed, genuinely amused as well as touched. But she explained that the law required children to pursue an education till they were at least sixteen. And, in any case, she further hoped I would go on to college.*

*"Well, then can you at least teach me how to make dinner for everybody? That would help you a little bit, wouldn't it?"*

*She leaned over and hugged me tight.*

*Less than a year later, I got the job.*

*"Compliments to the chef," Dad said cheerfully after my maiden effort.*

*It gave me the creeps.*

WHENEVER DAD WAS *in a "good mood" at dinner time, he would interrogate Chaz and me at length about our schoolwork and social activities. This would make us both squirm, so I got the idea of turning the tables and encouraging him to talk about what he had written that day. For even if it were not actually committed to paper yet, he would have pondered his topic—"The Concept of the Hero"—and come up with ideas worth hearing.*

*Indeed, years later in college, I got an "A" for a paper comparing Achilles and King Lear that was practically a carbon copy of one of Dad's more stimulating evening lectures.*

*I'm glad I was able to catch a glimpse of how inspiring a teacher he once must have been, and after a while began to understand the tortuous retreat he had made from life. Yet being a so-called expert on world literature, he was so daunted by the greatness of the classics that he ultimately all but gave up hope of producing anything worthwhile. What a waste.*

---

EVEN AT A YOUNG AGE, *my brother was already aware of the unorthodox nature of our household.*

*"Why doesn't he go to an office like other dads?"*

*"His office is in his mind. Don't you see that?"*

*"Not really," he confessed. "I mean, does his mind pay him any money?"*

*The kid was getting on my nerves.*

*"Shut up and either do your homework or peel some potatoes."*

*"How come you get to boss me around?" he complained.*

*"Just lucky, I guess." There was no point in sharing with him my feelings of guilt that he got saddled with me as a parental substitute.*

*While things were simmering on the stove or—to be more truthful—defrosting, I'd squeeze in a quick half hour at the piano. It was a welcome escape.*

*I wish there had been time in those years to go out for a sport. For I sometimes missed the fellowship of sweaty jocks that characterized early adolescence in Dearborn. And yet it was some compensation that, when I reached high school, I played for all the assemblies and was about the only guy who could compete with the jocks for the best girls.*

*For the piano was my unassailable fortress over which I reigned, a supreme and solitary monarch. It was a source of indescribable—almost physical—joy.*

IN OUR HOUSE *dinner was usually brief—how long does it take to eat macaroni and cheese? Dad would dematerialize with the last spoonful, leaving a word of praise for the bill of fare, and his sons to clean the kitchen.*

After Chaz and I cleared the dishes, we sat down at the table and I would help him with his math.

He was having problems at school, apparently being obstreperous and not paying attention. His teacher, Mr. Porter, had already written one letter home, which my father had intercepted, and its contents had put him in a state of high dudgeon. He chose to deal with it personally.

"What's all this about, Chaz?"

"Nothing, nothing," my brother protested. "The guy just picks on me, that's all."

"Ah," Dad remarked. "I thought so. Some arrogant Philistine. Well, I'll have to go in and set him straight."

I desperately tried to dissuade him:

"No, Dad, you can't."

"I beg your pardon, Matthew?" he addressed me with eyebrow raised. "I'm still the head of this family. As a matter of fact, I think I'll see this Mr. Porter tomorrow."

I was really worried and told Mom when she arrived home late from the hospital.

"Oh God," she groaned, clearly at the end of her tether. "We can't have him doing that."

"How can you stop him?"

She didn't answer. But later that evening, Chaz appeared in his pajamas when I was in my room studying. He motioned to me to be quiet and come out on the landing.

We stood there in the darkness like two castaways on a raft as we listened to our parents bickering acrimoniously.

"For heaven's sake," Mom complained angrily. "Don't make things worse than they are."

*"I'm his father, dammit. This oaf is picking on him and I won't have it."*

*"I'm not so sure it's quite the way Chaz described it. Anyway, let me handle it."*

*"I already said I'd take care of this matter, Joanne."*

*"I think it's best left to me, Henry," she said firmly.*

*"And why, may I ask?"*

*"Please, don't make me spell it out."*

*There was a chastened silence, and then I heard Dad's voice turn solicitous.*

*"You're looking tired, Joanne. Why don't you sit down and let me make you a drink."*

*"No!"*

*"I meant cocoa. Hell, it's the least I can do."*

*"No, Henry," she pronounced, at last revealing some of the enormous bitterness rising against the dam of her devotion to us. "I'm afraid it's the most you can do."*

*In the loneliness that permeated every corner of our house, I could barely see the outline of my little brother's face as he looked up to me for reassurance.*

*This time I could find nothing to say.*

# FOUR

SILVIA AND I were both yawning the next day. François tried all morning to catch my eye, but I deftly avoided his gaze. Let him leapfrog to whatever conclusion made him happy.

For her part, Dr. Dalessandro was back to her schoolmarm disguise, giving nothing away.

I thought I caught her sneaking me a smile, but it might have been wishful thinking. I couldn't wait to speak to her.

Our guest lecturer on typhus, Professor Jean-Michel Gottlieb of the famous La Salpêtrière hospital, specialized in "ancient diseases"—the ones most people think have long been eliminated from the face of the earth. Like smallpox or plague. Or leprosy, which still has millions of sufferers in Africa and India.

Moreover, he gently reminded us that, as we were chatting comfortably in Paris, there were more cases of tuberculosis in the world than at any previous time in human history.

In case I ever doubted my decision to join Médecine Internationale, Gottlieb was a living, eloquent reaffirmation. I thought I was a real doctor, but I had never in my life treated a case of smallpox. Even the most destitute welfare patients I had seen in America were *vaccinated*. And, except for the baby of an illegal couple from Guatemala, I had never seen a case of infantile polio either.

The Declaration of Independence may hold as self-evident that all men are created equal. But the tragic global truth is that beyond the industrial nations, untold numbers of the poorest people on our planet are denied basic human *health* rights.

And I think that's what made me so proud at the prospect of using my skills in the Third World. Here we would be not only curing people who had previously perished for lack of treatment, but also bringing miracles of *preventive* medicine, in the form of inoculations discovered by scientists from Jenner to Jonas Salk in a century that had not yet reached them.

During our especially abbreviated lunch break, Silvia and I did not join the eager beavers milling around Gottlieb, squeezing him to the last drop.

"Enjoying the lecture?" I inquired.

"Very much," she smiled. "Fortunately I spent last night with a young doctor who knew all the latest work on typhus."

I was just going to ask her about her plans for *that* evening when François banged his pointer on the ground and commanded us to resume work immediately.

Thus I had to endure an entire afternoon of exotic germs till I would learn my fate.

At precisely five o'clock, Professor Gottlieb concluded his presentation and wished us all good luck.

As I was sorting out the chaos of a day's worth of notes, Silvia came up, casually put her arm on my shoulder and asked, "Will you play for me tonight? I promise we'll study afterwards."

"On one condition," I stipulated. "That I take you to dinner in between."

"That's not a condition, that's a pleasure. When should we meet?"

"The hotel lobby at seven o'clock."

"Fine. How do I dress?"

"Very nicely," I riposted. "See you."

She gave me one of those backward *ciao* waves and plunged into her waiting cluster of admirers for the homeward parade.

WHEN I CAUGHT SIGHT of her that evening, I was not sure what, if anything, she had "changed" in her outfit. Then, on closer inspection, I noticed that her jeans were black instead of blue, her sweatshirt did not have any company logo and seemed to fit a little tighter. And she was, by her standards anyway, bejeweled: a small pearl necklace.

My own sartorial appearance was enhanced by a light blue sweater I had bought that afternoon in Galeries Lafayette.

After kissing me on both cheeks she immediately inquired if I had remembered our homework. I pointed to my flight bag and indicated that it did not contain my dirty laundry.

As we started out the door, she remarked matter-of-factly, "I've booked the Hotel Lutetia."

"Sorry," I declared, asserting my independence. "*I've* reserved Le Petit Zinc. I told you this way my—"

"No conflict, Matthew. The hotel is just for your concert."

What? The most elegant address in the whole arrondissement? I did not know whether to be flattered or annoyed. But I decided to withhold judgment and take her hand as we walked toward the Boulevard Raspail.

Still, by the time we reached the sumptuous lobby, I was beginning to feel distinctly uncomfortable. And I was downright intimidated when I entered the enormous high-ceilinged, multi-mirrored ballroom with a grand piano standing propped open at the far end.

"Did you rent an audience too?" I said, only half-joking.

"Don't be silly. And I didn't 'rent' this place either."

"You mean we're trespassing?"

"No. I simply phoned and asked the hotel manager's permission very nicely. The moment he heard who you were, he agreed right away."

"And who am I?"

"A passionate pianist for Médicine Internationale about to go abroad, where he'll be thousands of miles from the nearest keyboard. He was very impressed by your dedication."

My mood changed from minor to major. And I felt genuinely honored. I was suddenly consumed with the desire to play the hell out of that piano.

On a table nearby stood a tray with a bottle of white wine and two glasses.

"You?" I asked her.

She shook her head and observed, "There's a card."

I opened the envelope and read:

*Dear Doctors,*

*Enjoy your musical evening and know that people every-
where admire the "harmony" you are bringing to the less fortu-
nate of the world.*

*Bon voyage à vous deux.*

*Louis Bergeron*
MANAGER

"What did you tell him, Silvia? That I was Albert Schweitzer?"

She laughed.

"What makes you think you aren't?"

"You're about to find out."

I sat down and began to run my fingers over the keys. The dummy keyboard seemed to have served its purpose well.

"Hey," I remarked with pleasure. "It's just been tuned."

With my audience of one seated comfortably in a nearby chair, I began with Bach's Prelude No. 21 in B-flat—a deceptively easy piece. A good way of warming up without screwing up. Throughout, except for four measures, the master used but a single note at a time in each hand. Yet characteristically it was the right note.

When I first placed my hands on the keys, I felt a kind of shiver. I had not touched a piano in nearly three weeks and there was an almost sensual yearning to reunite with the instrument. I had not re-alized how much it was a part of my very being.

As I continued to play I became less and less a physical presence and more a part of the music itself.

I had not thought out a program in advance. I just let my psyche lead my hands. And at that moment they felt like exploring Mozart's

C minor sonata, K. 457. Feeling *allegro molto,* I launched into the octaves that crisply set out the tonality of the piece.

I was so hypnotically involved, I forgot Silvia was there. And gradually I ceased to be a player and became myself a listener—to someone else performing.

The piece could easily have been mistaken for Beethoven: powerful, eloquent and with strains of unworldly suffering.

By the time I was halfway through the slow movement, I was completely lost, like a spaceship floating among the stars.

Unaware of how much time had passed, I felt myself slowly regaining consciousness, becoming aware of my surroundings. I was once again assuming command of the music, and played the last few notes with a controlled passion. I let my head drop, emotionally depleted.

I don't know about Silvia, but I felt wonderful.

She did not say a word. But instead walked over, put a hand on either side of my face, and kissed my forehead.

A few minutes later, we were walking toward the restaurant. The Boulevard St. Michel was now dark and the sound of laughter, the most human of music, filtered from the cafés and bistros into the street. And yet she still had not offered the slightest verbal comment.

WE SELECTED OUR MEAL from the array of sea creatures displayed below and then went upstairs, where the waiter opened a bottle of house red for us. Silvia picked up her glass, but did not drink. She seemed lost in thought. At last she began awkwardly:

"Matthew, I don't know quite how to say this. But I come from a world where anything can be bought." She paused and then, leaning over the table, said with fire, *"Except what you just did."*

I did not know how to respond.

"You play like an angel. You could be a professional."

"No," I corrected her. "I'm an amateur in the truest sense of the word."

"But you could have been."

I shrugged. "Maybe, maybe not. But the point is, you can't play Bach to a child with TB until you make him well enough to hear it. I mean, that's why we're going to Eritrea, isn't it?"

"Of course," she said a trifle hesitantly. "It's just that I thought—I mean—you seem to have so much more going for you."

I suddenly got the sense that she was troubled with ambivalent feelings about taking this momentous step in her life. Perhaps understandably. For she would be going to one of the few places on earth where FAMA and its products were totally unknown.

IT WAS ELEVEN O'CLOCK when we set up shop at a table in the Café de Flore. We ordered coffee and began working through the next day's diseases.

As we should have expected, François, who always held court from a booth in the back, came over to see what we were doing.

He glanced at our papers and then addressed me with mock disdain, "You really disappoint me, Matthew."

"What do you mean?"

"Quite simply that if I were out with a creature as lovely as *La Dalessandro*, I wouldn't be wasting my time studying epidemiology."

"Buzz off, François," Silvia responded with mock annoyance.

And he retreated.

IT TOOK US NEARLY two hours to get through the complex material for the next day, which included a lot of statistics.

Silvia finally declared us ready. "Shall we switch to decaffeinated and have a nightcap?"

"Yeah, of course, why not. Especially since it's your round."

It had been a long evening, exhilarating but exhausting. I looked forward to hugging my pillow.

"I just thought of something," Silvia commented as we were packing up our gear. "The director of our Japanese division just sent my father a tiny new tape recorder. You could make some cassettes that we could take along and play in Asmara."

"I've got a better idea," I countered. "Since we won't have anything to do with our money, why don't we buy some real performers, like Ashkenazy or Daniel Barenboim—"

"I prefer you," she persisted.

"Try and break the habit," I advised.

We left the café and began to walk slowly back to the hotel.

"How did you get started in the first place?" she inquired. "I mean with the piano."

"Do you want the long version or the short version?"

"I'm in no rush. Why don't I show you the baguette factory so we can buy our own breakfast?" She smiled.

*WHEN I WAS A KID, I had this persistent fantasy that my Dad would come to one of our school field days and beat all the other fathers in the hundred-yard dash. Needless to say, it never happened because he was always "under the weather" on the day of the competitions.*

*Sometimes he would still lurch over and make an appearance, but then he'd sit on the side as a bemused observer, nipping secretly from his flask. So I never saw him physically active till that morning in the school* yard when, out of the corner of my eye, I caught sight of him at the gate. He seemed to be heading for Mr. Porter, my brother's math teacher.

I was trying to concentrate on playing half-court basketball when suddenly I heard Tommy Steadman shout, "Holy shit, Hiller, your Dad's fantastic."

I felt a sudden irrational thrill. I had never before derived any pride from my father. Unfortunately, my euphoria immediately evaporated. For what Tommy had so admired was the fact that my Dad had thrown a punch at Mr. Porter, catching him off balance and knocking him to the ground.

By the time I ran over, the victim had regained his footing and was shaking a menacing finger at my father.

"You'll hear from me, you drunken fool," he shouted loudly as he retreated into the school building.

My father stood there out of breath, with one of his triumphant grins. He noticed me and called out, "Hi, Matthew. Did you see me deck the wicked giant?"

My heart sank. I was humiliated beyond belief and longed to dissolve into water drops and seep into the ground.

"Dad, why did you do it? Mom begged you—" I stopped myself. "I mean, it'll only make things much worse for Chaz."

He bristled. "I'm sorry, son. But I couldn't let that Neanderthal persecute your brother. I think you should be proud of me. Come on, I'll take you two out to lunch."

"No, Dad," I said quietly. "We've still got four periods left. Why don't you go on home."

I sensed he wouldn't leave unless I took the initiative, so I kind of grabbed his arm and walked him towards the gate. I could feel the eyes of my classmates burning holes into my back and did not dare turn around.

Unfortunately, when we reached the exit, I caught sight of them. They were all standing and watching, conspicuously silent.

Somehow that made things worse. I knew that mockery was inevitable and dreaded the thought of coming across a cluster of kids sniggering at some later time.

I started back on the long, long road towards my peers, my gaze fixed firmly on the ground.

"Are you okay, Matthew?"

I looked up and was startled to find it was Mr. Porter. And he didn't seem to be angry with me.

"Yes, sir. I'm all right."

"Is he like that very often?"

I didn't know how to answer. Should I increase my shame by admitting that he was a chronic drunk? Or should I try to save some molecules of dignity?

"Now and then," I answered vaguely and walked slowly back to Tommy Steadman. "Hey, are we going to play ball?"

"Yeah, sure, Hiller. Sure."

And ironically, the thing that hurt the most about this multihurtful incident was that my friends were so nice. So horribly, painfully, pityingly nice.

FORTUNATELY, MY FATHER MADE no more such quixotic sallies into the real world. He thereafter remained at home, "working on his book" and railing against the injustice of the world.

At this point I myself was not too thrilled about the hand that Life *had dealt me. And my only release was in the evening when Chaz was squared away. Accommodatingly, he grew up swiftly, and soon was able to shift for himself and voluntarily retire to his room and study. This left me alone to practice the piano, which I would do for hours on end, pouring out my anger and invoking all the discipline my father lacked.*

*By the time I was in high school, I was too busy to sit and listen to his now rambling lectures and, besides, he finally pushed me too far.*

*I was sweating over Chopin's* Fantasie-Impromptu *late one evening, when he appeared somewhat unsteadily at the doorway and snapped, "I'm trying to work. Must you play so loud?"*

*I reflected for a moment, remembering Chaz upstairs grinding and not criticizing my volume. I then locked into my father's gaze and, losing my temper but not raising my voice, sternly answered, "Yes."*

*I turned back to the music and ignored him forever.*

I was quiet for a moment and then I said softly, "A little while after that he killed himself."

She grasped my arm tightly.

"Although he never went anywhere, he kept a car in the garage and he would sometimes go out, sit there and I guess fantasize that he was on the open road, heading for some destination. One day, in what I took to be the ultimate gesture of shutting out the world, he attached a hose to the exhaust pipe. . . ."

I looked at her and she was at a loss for words.

"Anyway, I don't often bring this up in conversation."

"No," she agreed. "You don't have to. It's just always there—behind a thin gauze of memory—waiting to emerge when you least expect it."

She understood, this girl. She *really* understood.

We walked the rest of the way in total silence.

When we reached the hotel, she kissed me quietly, squeezed my arm again, and then slipped off.

It was the depth of night, a time I always hated. Yet at that moment, I did not feel so utterly alone.

# FIVE

PARADOXICALLY, *my father's death, though a difficult period for us, was a kind of liberation.*

*It had been like watching a man teetering on a tightrope stretched across Niagara Falls. Though it took a while until he actually let go, his fate was clearly sealed from the moment he had begun to waver. The fall itself was almost an anticlimax.*

*I had to respect the minister for not delivering a saccharine eulogy. There was no nonsense about a great man torn from us tragically in the prime of life.*

*Rather, he spoke a few sentences about our common hope that Henry Hiller's troubled soul would find peace at last. And left it at that.*

*Curiously, it was far more of a comfort to hear the truth confirmed than to perpetuate a hypocritical myth.*

*Not surprisingly, little changed. Dad simply disappeared from the periphery of our existence, and we were left as the family unit we had already become without him before he died.*

*If anything, the pace of my life intensified. I was chosen to represent our school in the State Keyboard Competition and took second prize.*

*Whereas a year earlier I would have been ecstatic just to be invited, I was now disappointed that I had not won it all.*

*On the bus ride home, Mr. Adam, my teacher, consoled me by explaining that the gold medalist, Marisa Greenfield, had not really outplayed me musically, but rather outperformed me theatrically.*

*"She had the presence of a winner, looked confident and soulful when she walked on, and was completely caught up by the music."*

*"But I was all of those things, dammit."*

*"I know. But she was skillful enough to create a dramatic persona for the judges, whereas you were just your honest everyday self playing flawlessly. If the contestants had all played behind screens, you would have won hands down."*

*Marisa actually came over to me during the party afterward and suggested we collaborate on a concert of piano duets. I was flattered and probably should have followed up. But I wanted to go to med school and had lab sciences to take, not to mention the College Boards.*

*Still, we exchanged numbers and promised to keep in touch. She called one evening when I was out playing (developing my new dramatic flair) at the junior high school. I somehow never got around to phoning her back.*

*After a two-hour audition, the music department of the University of Michigan offered me a full scholarship. I was bowled over and sailed home from Ann Arbor on a cloud. But it really only sank in when I shared the news with my mother and brother.*

*In the ensuing celebration, I told Mom to take the money she had* been scrimping and saving for my education and get herself the new car she so badly needed. But she insisted that I not be penalized for my success and that I spend it on something that would bring me pleasure. The choice was obvious: a secondhand piano. On one of my reconnoitering visits I discovered an unusually tolerant landlady with a room for rent and a taste for classical music who allowed me to live with the instrument. ("Only for pity's sake, Matthew, no rock and roll, please.")

Not surprisingly, as the time for leaving home drew near, I had mixed feelings. A part of me felt uneasy about Mom and Chaz being without me. Another part was scared about me being without them.

MY NEXT FOUR YEARS RESONATED.

Though premed scientific courses were no doubt conceived to destroy the soul, majoring in music made mine indestructible. I explored beyond the keyboard into the riches of the orchestra. I fell in love with opera and so chose Italian to fulfill my language requirement. I could now listen to The Marriage of Figaro and understand how the librettist's skill enhanced the composer's art. Mozart alone was great. But Mozart and da Ponte—a divine banquet of the senses.

The course of my life had changed dramatically.

For as long as I could remember, I had been trudging through a dark labyrinth of work and worry. Now, at long last, I was on a sun-swept plain that stretched all the way to a blue and cloudless horizon. And I even discovered that these strange new feelings had a name: happiness.

My appearances as a soloist with various chamber groups made me something of a BMOC and added immeasurably to my confidence when introducing myself to the better-looking, intellectual coeds.

Yet the most significant event of my entire freshman year was meeting Evie.

She was warm and pretty in a fresh-faced sort of way, with short brown hair, an infectious smile and wide hazel eyes that always beamed with optimism. But, most important, she was an extremely talented cellist.

Ever since her childhood in Ames, Iowa, she had aspired to emulate her heroine, Jacqueline du Pré. We would listen to every record we could get our hands on of Jackie on the cello communing eloquently with her pianist-husband, Daniel Barenboim. We played them so often that we practically wore out the grooves in the LPs.

Although we spent almost every waking moment together, Evie was not a girlfriend in the romantic sense. It's just that we found in each other the qualities we both were looking for in a best pal.

She was already a sophomore when we met, and at first I suspected an ulterior motive in her friendliness toward a naive youngster like myself. I mean, cellists need accompanists, and the one thing I can do with the best of them is sight-read.

I guess at the time we didn't fully appreciate the uniqueness of our relationship. I mean, it started with Mozart and Bach and ended up with everything in the world. Call it the harmony of mutual understanding.

We confided things to one another that we would never have revealed to anyone else. Not just about how we felt about whom we were dating, but far more intimately the fact that we had both wrestled with the problem of what to do with the rest of our lives.

Mr. and Mrs. Webster were strongly against their daughter becoming a professional musician. They genuinely believed it was incompatible with marriage, which should be every girl's first career choice.

If her parents had their way, Evie would be at the local teachers' college, perhaps teach high school for a few years and then settle down with one of the nice professional boys returning to Ames with their diplomas.

"Are you telling me they don't understand what the cello means to you?" I asked.

She tried to shrug it off. "My mother is a nice person who honestly believes that my lifelong musical 'needs' should be more than satisfied by just singing in the choir on Sundays and doing Handel's Messiah every Christmas."

"So where did you get your love for the cello?"

"Aunt Lily, my mother's sister. She studied in Italy, toured Europe for a while with a trio and then came back and taught here till the day she died. She never married. From the time I was five she would take me to every concert within drivable distance—sometimes all the way to Des Moines. Part of the reason I admired virtuosi like Rubinstein and Heifetz was that they cared enough to trudge through winter storms to play for us hicks. When she died, Lily left me her cello and money specifically earmarked 'to further Evie's musical education.'"

"That's beautiful. You should name your first kid after her."

"I will," Evie smiled. "But only if it's a girl."

OF COURSE, NOT EVERY CONVERSATION we had was soul-searching. After all, we saw each other every day and we were bound to discuss ordinary things like term papers, football games or the upcoming Jean Cocteau Film Festival.

Nonetheless, Evie often had to disabuse her boyfriends about the nature of our relationship. Some were still not convinced even when she fixed me up with one or two of her more attractive friends. But I was too intoxicated with my music—and my newfound freedom—to be interested in anything long lasting.

And then there were those Saturday nights when, like two monastic devotees, we abjured the other collegiate pleasures—like beer and bowling—and simply remained in the special world we had created for ourselves, working on yet another piece of music.

The most "passionate" moments in those years were the times Evie and I spent practicing together. We shared so many hours that we went through almost every major work for piano and cello. I loved watching her unconsciously running her tongue across her bottom lip when she was concentrating on working out the fingering of a particularly difficult passage. Sometimes more than an hour would pass without our exchanging a spoken word. When you're playing with someone you really know, the communication becomes instinctive—too deep for ordinary conversation. It was an artistic experience that drew us into an even more intimate friendship.

Of course, we gave each other moral as well as musical support. One simultaneous occasion I can think of was when I accompanied her in Fauré's Sicilienne, which she had chosen for her degree recital in the spring of her senior year. I knew my part well enough to be able to sneak glances at the professors' faces and could tell she was making a really good impression.

As I predicted, she received a summa—and I received the longest, warmest embrace she had ever given me. I could still smell her perfume on my sweater the next morning.

I have always been grateful that she was there to help me during my big identity crisis, for, with each passing semester, I was coming closer and closer to an unavoidable crossroad.

Which path would I take?

The faculty weren't making it any easier. They seemed to be actively engaged in a tug-of-war, trying to pull me either toward music or medicine. I felt like I was being torn apart.

*Evie was the only person I could talk to about it. She did not push me one way or the other, but bolstered my confidence so that I could make a choice.*

*"You can make it as a pro," she asserted. "I mean, you've got the divine spark that makes the difference between a technical master and a virtuoso. You know that, Matt, don't you?"*

*I nodded. There was no question that I wanted to keep on playing music for the rest of my life. And yet a part of me could not imagine a life that did not somehow involve helping other people, giving something back—maybe a legacy from Mom.*

*Evie understood this too and tried very carefully not to influence me one way or another. She would sit there as a sympathetic audience to my endless argument with myself.*

THAT SUMMER WAS THE CRUCIBLE.

*While Evie was off at the Aspen Festival taking a cello master class with Roger Josephson, I slaved as an orderly in the University hospital.*

*I remember one night all during my shift on the pediatric ward there was this comatose girl who seemed to be whimpering. I reported it to the nurses, who insisted she was drugged to the eyeballs and could not be feeling any pain.*

*Nonetheless, when I went off duty I went over, sat down and took the child's hand. She suddenly went quiet.*

*I remained at her bedside till nearly daybreak. The girl must have been aware that I had been with her all the time, because when she awoke she gave me a little smile and said, "Thank you, Doctor."*

*I called Evie and told her I had made up my mind.*

*"I'm really glad, Matthew."*

*"That I'm going into medicine?"*

*"No,"* she said fondly. *"That you've finally decided."*

So was I.

IN THE MIDDLE OF HER SENIOR YEAR, *Evie received the good news that Josephson's intercession on her behalf had succeeded in winning her a scholarship to Juilliard.*

*She begged me to apply to med school in New York so that we could keep playing together. I thought about it. The idea was tempting—even though Chaz had been accepted to Michigan and would be arriving on campus the following fall.*

*Anyway, I went to the medical adviser's office, got an armful of brochures for New York and other more exotic spots and began to study them.*

*At last the time came for Evie to leave. I guess most good friends would have gone out for a farewell meal or something, but we had other ideas about how we wanted to spend our last evening together. We went down to our favorite practice room at around six P.M. and were still there at midnight when Ron, the janitor, came to evict us. After we explained the special nature of the occasion, he said we could finish whatever we were in the midst of, while he locked up the rest of the place.*

*And so we concluded with César Franck's Sonata in A, which Jacqueline du Pré and Daniel Barenboim had recently recorded.*

*The music was full of sadness and yearning, and we both attacked it with a depth of feeling that surpassed all other moments we had ever played together.*

I TOOK HER TO THE AIRPORT *the next morning. We hugged, then she was gone.*

*I drove home in a very empty car.*

————

THAT SEPTEMBER, *the prodigal brother arrived in Ann Arbor, all grown up and ready to live.*

*Of course, his idea of living was, no doubt, strongly conditioned by the psychic uncertainties of our childhood. He seemed in an enormous hurry to establish domestic stability.*

*To prove this, before he even chose a major, he chose a steady girlfriend.*

*In a matter of months he and Ellen Morris, a freckle-faced guitar-playing classmate, were living happily together on the top floor of a two-family house in Plainfield, a twenty-five minute bus ride from the university.*

*Meanwhile, I was busy writing my senior thesis in music, while suffering through organic chemistry—the scientific equivalent of a bad toothache.*

*Several nights a week (at eleven P.M., when the rates changed) Evie and I would talk on the phone. It was not as satisfying as our "live" conversations—and certainly not as good as making music together—but it was still nice to hear her views on everything from my dates to my dissertation. She thought more of the latter than the former. She even felt it might be publishable.*

*I was writing on the single inspired year in which Verdi wrote both* Il Trovatore *and* La Traviata *(1852–1853). I could see the similarities in style and his evolution as an orchestrator. It was almost like getting inside the composer's head. Both readers obviously shared Evie's opinion because they gave me an "A+."*

WHEN MOM CAME TO VISIT US *for Thanksgiving, she brought an unexpected surprise. His name was Malcolm Hearn, M.D. My hunch that someone had recently come into her personal life turned out to be accurate.*

*A divorced surgeon with grown children, Malcolm not only seemed like a warm, solid guy with a sense of humor (and a world view at the antipodes of Dad's), but he was also something of a musician, a first tenor, to be exact. And a real one, who could hit high "C" without having to cheat and go falsetto. This quality alone would have made him a sought-after guest at any choral event. Mal already was the star of the hospital barbershop quartet. And to hear him sing the soaring upper counterpoint to "You Gotta Have Heart" would bring a smile to the sourest of listeners. Most important, he seemed really fond of Mom, who would now have a genuine second chance at the brass ring of happiness.*

EVIE WAS REALLY PLEASED *to hear about Malcolm. ("A surgeon, a nice guy and high 'C'? That's too good to be true!")*

*I told her she could make up her own mind when she met him at Christmas.*

*"Uh, I was working up the courage to tell you, Matthew. I'm afraid I'm not going to be able to come out after all. Roger and I—"*

*"Roger?" I asked with an irrational pang of jealousy. "Are you referring to Maestro Josephson?"*

*"Uh, yes. Actually, he's the guy who just answered the phone."*

*"Hey—" I said, suddenly self-conscious. "You should have told me I was disturbing."*

*"You never disturb me. Besides, I told him all about us. Listen, why don't you join us at Sugarbush for a week of skiing?"*

*"Gosh, I wish I could. But I'm snowed under with work. I'll barely make it home for one day. Anyway, Merry Christmas."*

*I hung up feeling like a stupid ass. I had given Evie holiday greetings an entire month too early.*

I STAYED IN ANN ARBOR *for med school. This way I could see Chaz and Ellen regularly, even after they were married (she started her teaching degree while he got a job as an executive trainee for Blue Cross).*

*Marriage was epidemic that year. In August Evie and Roger also tied the knot at Tanglewood, where he was playing the Dvořák under Zubin Mehta. Fortunately, I came down two days early because, while Roger was off at his bachelor party, Evie had a fit of what I can only describe as cold feet. ("I mean, Matt, he's so famous and—so grown up. Why does he want a kid like me?")*

*I managed to convince her that a guy like Roger was astute enough to appreciate what a special person she was. For that matter, whoever married her would know he was the luckiest guy in the world. The inevitable crisis was long forgotten by the time the corks and flashbulbs popped.*

*As for me, the best part of the festivities was the concert by some of the guests after the ceremony. It seemed as if half my cassette collection was there in person.*

*I went home and plunged into the world of doctoring. Some time that fall, Evie dropped out of Juilliard to be able to travel with Roger and gradually our worlds drifted apart.*

EVEN WHEN HE WAS *a full-fledged husband, Chaz and I continued to meet on Sunday nights for beer and fraternal conversation.*

*He still had the knack for asking annoying questions.*

"Are you sorry you didn't marry Evie when you had the chance?" he inquired naively.

"It would never have worked. We were just like brother and sister."

"Then why are you so miserable?"

"I'm not miserable, Chaz. I'm just nervous about my interview for Africa."

"Africa?" he reacted incredulously. "Ah, you must be joining the Foreign Legion to try and forget her."

"Cut it out," I rebuked him. And then confessed that I had applied for a job with Médecine Internationale, an organization setting up clinics in hot spots of the Third World, treating victims of poverty and politics.

"Hey, that sounds right up your altruistic alley. Is it dangerous?"

"That depends on where they send you. I'm hoping to go to Eritrea. There's a civil war going on there. But from what they tell me, neither side is stupid enough to shoot at doctors."

"Well, just be sure to wear 'M.D.' plates on your pajamas," Chaz joked with manifest concern. "Anyway, when do you hear?"

"Next week, after the interview in Paris."

"You mean you've reached the interview stage and didn't tell your own brother?"

"I thought if I was going to fail, I would do it in private."

"Come on, Matt. You never fail."

"Well," I said with a smile. "This could be my big chance."

# SIX

*Milano, September 1953*

THEY STOOD in order of rank. God first. The Virgin Mary. And then the baby.

The more important guests who had gathered in Milan's Duomo were already on familiar terms with the first two. But the infant had just been born.

She was the daughter of Gian Battista Dalessandro, the owner of FAMA, Italy's largest conglomerate. And this was her social debut.

As the prime minister held the child and the cardinal chanted the Latin words that baptized her Silvia Maria Dalessandro, her mother, Caterina, whispered to her husband, "I wish I believed in God so I could thank Him."

He smiled broadly and embraced his wife.

"He exists, *carina*. How else could we have found each other?"

Though the dignitaries had flown in from distant corners of the world, in a sense the one who had traveled the farthest was Mario Rinaldi. For Gian Battista's rival and best friend had been born in a small southern Italian backwater and had not owned a pair of shoes until he was ten. Now he was the chairman of Gruppo METRO (Metalmeccanica Torinese), the second-richest man in Italy, whose company produced items ranging from hair dryers to helicopters—not to mention the tires for every car that came off the FAMA assembly lines.

Although yet again the occasion belonged to Gian Battista, with industrial potentates orbiting him like deferential planets, Mario had one consolation: even after two marriages, and for all his money, Gian Battista had not been able to buy a son and heir. And that was something *he* had.

As the prelate sprinkled water on the infant's head, Mario whispered to the darkly handsome teenager at his side, "She is going to be your wife."

Young Nico, all of sixteen, could not tell whether it was a command or a prediction.

THE HEIR TO THE METRO FORTUNE reached his majority never having worked a single day in his life—and never intending to.

To please his father Nico had gone through the motions of a university education, subsidizing a number of needy students who wrote his papers and even took his exams. He had better things to do.

Since childhood he had been in love with speed: on the ground, in the air and in the water. This omnivorous passion afforded year-round opportunities for risking his life.

In the summer he moored his racing boat in the Nice harbor and would expropriate the palatial guest house at his parents' estate with an ever-changing crowd of friends in tow.

Though her father had tried to develop in Silvia an instinctive wariness of strangers, he did not regard the son of his Riviera neighbor as an outsider. Nico was, among other things, Gian Battista's favorite tennis partner and every year they battled each other in a marathon summer-long tournament. Neither liked to lose.

Silvia would always sit courtside and stand up periodically to "announce" the score in English, French and Italian.

Nico's latest *principessa*, the luxuriant Simona Gattopardo, was charmed.

"Would you like to play tennis with me sometime?" she asked.

"For how much?" the little girl asked ingenuously. "Nico and Papa always play for really big money."

"She just said that to throw you off your game," Nico's voice suddenly interrupted.

"Your niece is very sweet."

"She's not my niece. She's my pal," he offered, draping his arm around Simona as they walked off toward the terrace.

Silvia watched them go with a pang she did not yet realize was jealousy.

And naturally Nico was too involved in his own pursuits to notice that the little girl adored him.

ONE WINTER HER FATHER AND MARIO took Silvia to see Nico race his bobsled in Cortina d'Ampezzo. Watching her hero and his teammate fly around the track, she felt that portion of her self, normally hemmed in and suffocated by bodyguards, take wing as well. For, in a very real sense, he was living out her own fantasies of freedom.

Toward the end of the afternoon, his sled hit a patch of water, spun out of control and crashed, rolling over several times. The brakeman fell free, apparently unhurt.

Silvia burst into tears. Gian Battista picked her up to comfort her.

At the first-aid station the medics made a tentative inventory of Nico's broken bones and prepared him for the helicopter ride to Milan.

"Will you be all right?" Silvia asked solicitously.

"Of course, *carina,*" he replied with bravado. "I'm indestructible."

GIAN BATTISTA VISITED the younger Rinaldi in his spacious top-floor hospital room and reported to his wife and daughter.

"I think he's going to be in there for quite a few months."

"Maybe the doctors will transplant some sense into his head," Caterina remarked with disapproval. "Then maybe he'll find something worthwhile to do with himself."

"I think he's already looking. His list of visitors looks like a *Who's Who* of the business world. I think that's where he'll compete for his gold medals from now on."

"Good. It's about time he settled down. What's he waiting for?"

At that point Silvia, who had been playing quietly nearby, chirped up, "Me."

IN THE SPRING OF 1964, Caterina Dalessandro was abducted by a revolutionary group and held for an obscenely large ransom.

In a swift and uncharacteristic burst of efficiency, the Italian police closed off all the Dalessandro bank accounts so they would be unable to surrender to the terrorists' demands.

At this point the Rinaldis, father and son, proved their friendship.

While Mario flew to London for the dollars, Nico sped to Lugano to bring back the Swiss francs to enable Gian Battista to meet the kidnappers' demands.

Unfortunately the *carabinieri,* who had been tapping the phones, reached the terrorists before the money did.

And in the exchange of fire that followed, Caterina was shot dead.


FROM THE MOMENT GIAN BATTISTA received the news, he closed himself in his room, unable to face the world.

Although he knew his daughter needed him, he did not have the emotional strength to respond. It was like living behind a wall of glass. He could see but not touch other people.

The task of comforting Silvia fell to Nico.

The day before the funeral, while his father was alone with Gian Battista in his study, the young Rinaldi strolled up to the playroom.

The place was empty, although toys and dolls were spilled everywhere.

He then wandered downstairs and into the garden, past the swimming pool, motionless and silent, and then the equally deserted tennis court.

At last, looking ahead toward the fountain, he caught sight of Silvia seated on a bench, staring into space. Her governess, Miss Turner, was trying to distract her by reading aloud.

The ten-year-old child wore a look of utter desolation.

Even when she finally noticed him, she neither smiled nor ran to his arms.

Nodding to her companion, he sat down next to the little girl and began to speak softly.

"Silvia, I can't tell you how sorry I am. I mean, for your mother—and for you."

There was a moment of silence. Then she answered, her voice hollow:

"The world seems like such a horrible place."

"Yeah, I can see life must be unbearable right now. But you can't give up. You know what your mother would have wanted."

She shook her head. The look on her face reflected as much perplexity as pain.

"Nico, my father won't talk to me. Did I do something wrong?"

"Just give him a little time. He's coping the best way he can."

She looked at him quizzically. "Do you believe in God?"

"Don't they teach you about Him in school?"

"Yes, but I'm asking you. Do you believe?"

"Well, sometimes."

"I only wish I could ask Him what Mama did that was so bad that He punished her."

Yeah, Nico thought to himself. This is definitely one of those times when I don't believe.

He looked out toward the horizon and said as casually as possible, "I don't know about you, but I'm cold. Let's all go inside and get something nice and warm to drink."

At first she did not reply.

"Come on, pal." He extended his hand to her. "Do it for me."

She slowly rose and the three of them walked back into the house.

———

THE BURIAL WAS PRIVATE but the tragedy was mercilessly public.

A plague of paparazzi with telescopic lenses stood beyond the cemetery walls on hastily constructed platforms, their cameras feeding like carrion on the victims' grief.

The mourners wound their way slowly behind the coffin. Nico held Silvia's hand as they walked a step behind Gian Battista and Mario Rinaldi.

At the end of the service, as the dignitaries began to leave, Silvia remained beside the open grave and whispered, "Goodbye, Mama."

Then she turned, took Nico's hand again, and walked away.

# SEVEN

SUDDENLY THE ENTIRE population of Paris was reduced to only Silvia and me.

We sat next to each other all day in class and in the evenings dined together in different local bistros. Then, after ploughing through the assignments for the next day, we would close our books and just talk.

If there was a single quality that characterized Silvia, it was passion.

She was deeply committed to being a good doctor, loved opera and was fanatic about professional basketball, embracing every aspect of life with enthusiasm. As I think of it now she evoked in me the ecstatic feeling of the final chorus of Beethoven's Ninth: "Joy, divine radiance, daughter of Elysium. . . ."

Somehow, neither the onus of excessive wealth

nor the bruises of a painful childhood appeared to have handicapped her in any way.

Or so it seemed at first.

She had obviously led a sheltered existence and had few, if any, intimate friends. For she was artlessly candid and made no effort to disguise the complexities that lay beneath her flawless exterior. Yet it was interesting how often she mentioned her mother.

"When she married my father, Mama was the editor of *La Mattina,* Italy's largest morning paper. But from the moment they met they hardly spent a night apart. After I was born, she converted a wing of the house into offices and with daredevil motorcycle messengers, endless charm—and a very loud voice—she ran the whole show from home. And yet she wasn't like those women who are so wrapped up in their careers they have no room for their kids. Day or night she was always there when I needed her."

From the vantage point of time and grief it was hard to tell whether this was a real memory or an idealization.

"How did you manage afterward?"

"Well, there was my father," she said softly. Her tone revealed more familial loyalty than genuine conviction. She then confessed quietly, "Although he needed my support even more than I needed his. Actually, Papa's never really recovered. He's still trying to work himself to death. I worry about him."

"But who worried about you? Who played with you? Who took you to school?"

"Different people. I don't remember anyone in particular. It didn't seem like a big deal at the time, since all of them wore the same uniform."

At this point I could not suppress the comment, "I've always believed that there are two things you can't have someone else do for you—get a haircut and be a parent."

She smiled. A knowing smile of assent. "Sarah Conrad, my best friend at school, used to practice psychiatry without a license. In her unauthorized opinion, I had a major case of parental deprivation. According to her, if I don't talk to a shrink, I'll probably mess up every relationship in my life."

Not with *me*, I thought to myself. And tried to dispel this unexpected display of vulnerability.

"Come on, Silvia. There are exceptions to every rule. I mean, there are people who come from large, close-knit families who are just as screwed up as the loners. I cite, as but one classic example, the Old Woman Who Lived in a Shoe."

"Yes," Silvia laughed, and then quoted, "'she whipped them all soundly and put them to bed.'"

"Right. By the way, how does that sound in Italian?"

"I don't know, Nico read it to me in English."

"Ah, Nico."

"Yes. He also taught me how to play tennis. And chess. And he took me to the circus."

"Then I guess you're going to marry him," I stated, masking the sinking pessimism about my own chances.

"What makes you say that? I mean, that was ages ago. He's a hundred years old now."

"To begin with, he's not. He's young enough for you to play with and old enough to look up to. But most of all, he always seems to have been there. And that's very important to you, isn't it?"

She nodded, extinguishing the final sparks of hope still flickering within me.

"You're right to a certain extent," she conceded. "I mean, he was really wonderful during the period I refer to as my 'incarceration.'"

"What do you mean by that?"

"Understandably, after what happened to Mama my father was obsessed with protecting me. I mean, he pulled me out of school and had me tutored at home. You can imagine what kind of security checks his people did on those poor bastards.

"And as far as my social life was concerned," she added facetiously, "some people may think it's posh to have their own movie theater at home complete with popcorn. But it's not so good when every weekend you and the same three or four kids are the only audience. I was fourteen before I discovered that the *least* important part of the movie is what happens on the screen. I desperately missed other people."

"How did you finally get away? Was that with Sir Nico's help too?"

"Stop teasing," she chided. "But, as a matter of fact, he was always encouraging me to study abroad. Still, I couldn't really leave my father until he was on his feet again."

How strange, the parental instinct coming from a child.

"And then I finally decided that if he was ever to rejoin the human race I had to go. I mean, I thought that if I left him on his own, he'd be forced to start looking for somebody else.

"Anyway, England was the only country whose security he approved of. Naturally, the school would have to be Catholic. So, this pretty much boiled down to St. Bartholomew's in Wiltshire.

"I was happy there, although it took me a while to get used to all that religious stuff. Besides meeting my best friend, Sarah, and learning to play every sport known to man, I got a hell of an education. But every morning and evening, the only thing I ever prayed for was that next Visitors' Day, Papa would come with a nice new lady on his arm." She then added wistfully, "But he never did.

"That meant I had to spend summers with him in Italy. I hated the idea of his living by himself. I didn't get to see many people my own age, but Papa and I had some lovely times together. I know he enjoyed taking me along when he visited the factories. He was so proud of me. Actually, it was the only time he seemed to come out of his shell and be really animated. He would break into one of his rare smiles as he introduced me to everybody. I kind of liked it too. The workers seemed genuinely fond of him."

That fact was corroborated in an article I had recently come across in *Le Monde*. It mentioned her father as one of the pioneering northern Italian industrialists to offer low-cost housing for his self-exiled workers from the south who otherwise would have had to leave their families back home.

"But my worst vivid memories are of the weekends we spent together in La Locanda, a little *alberghetto* in the backwoods of Tuscany. It was for upper-crust Italians from Milan and Torino who weren't loud and flashy."

"In that case it must have been really small," I joked.

She laughed. "You're right, Matthew, that's why this place was so special. Despite its simple name, 'The Inn' was quiet and elegant. At night they served dinner in a garden filled with the smell of jasmine. To my teenage eyes, anyway, the men all seemed so handsome, with their tans and white linen suits. But none was better-looking than my father. The women wore the most fashionable but understated dresses and there was this little trio that played for dancing."

"Piano, drums and violin, right?"

"Yes, my musician friend," she smiled.

"I kind of figured that the fiddle would make it romantic."

"It was," she nodded, "but unfortunately not for a fifteen-year-old and her daddy."

I'm not so sure, I thought to myself.

"Every summer I kept hoping we would meet someone for Papa."

I found myself strangely touched at the thought of a teenage Silvia circling the dance floor with her father, while discreetly scanning the tables for eligible widows.

"One evening there were two ladies at the table right next to ours. The younger woman was dark, attractive, the perfect age. And they were sitting close enough for me to notice that she wasn't wearing a ring. All through dinner they seemed to glance at us and whisper to one another. Just before they served the coffee, the older lady got up, kissed the younger one goodnight and disappeared.

"Hey, this is getting interesting. Who made the next move?"

"I did, naturally. I got a sudden headache, excused myself and insisted that Papa stay and finish dinner.

"As I left the dining room, I glanced back and saw my father reach for his cigarette case. He was obviously not in a hurry. It was the moment I had been waiting for for so long. I couldn't sleep or even read. I spent at least an hour at my window, craning to get a glimpse of the restaurant to see if they were dancing. The next morning I woke up and even fantasized about her being at breakfast with us on my father's terrace. She wasn't there, but he was in such a good mood I felt certain he had made plans for lunch. I couldn't wait that long, so I asked him straight out what he thought of the beautiful brunette who had sat nearby the night before."

She paused and shook her head with dismay.

"Don't tell me," I suggested. "He preferred blondes."

"No, you idiot. He hadn't even noticed her at all."

"I GUESS I TALKED TOO MUCH, HUH?" Silvia said apologetically. It was close to one A.M. and we were standing in the empty lobby of "St. Fleabag" (another of the sobriquets I invented for the dump we lived in).

"Not at all," I answered sincerely. "How else can you get to know a person?"

"But knowing isn't synonymous with liking," she ventured.

"Silvia, in your case it couldn't mean anything else."

We exchanged goodnight kisses on the cheek and she took the elevator to her room. I, incorrigible American that I am, did my daily exercise, walking up the creaking stairway to my tenth- (or so it felt at that hour) floor garret. As I climbed I thought—unless I was too drunk on hope—that there was meaning in her last ostensibly innocuous remark. Nico had not won her yet. I still had a chance.

THE NEXT NIGHT IN THE CAFÉ DE FLORE, after we had covered the last item on our agenda—a thorough study of the onset, development and cure of schistosomiasis, a common blood infection gotten from contact with contaminated water—we ordered a carafe of dry white and went through what by now was a familiar ritual: reopening our psychic family albums.

We talked about the things that attracted us to medicine in the first place.

"To tell the truth," Silvia said, "I can't remember a time when, at some level, I didn't want to be a doctor. I mean, I guess it started as far back as Giorgio."

"Who was he?"

She hunched over the table as she always did when she was sharing her innermost thoughts with me. And tonight, thanks to the cut of her sweater, I could not avoid a glance at her lovely breasts as she told me about Giorgio Rizutto.

"He was my first 'boyfriend.' We were both seven years old. He was a skinny kid, with black saucer eyes, a lot smaller than the rest of us. During recess, while the other boys ran and fooled around, he would sit on the sidelines all alone. I'd go over and keep him company.

"But he could never come to our house and play. It turned out that every evening after school he had to go to the hospital for dialysis."

She took a deep breath.

"Damn. Even after all this time, it's still tough to speak about it. Apparently he didn't have much longer to live. My father offered to pay for him to have one of those new kidney transplants in America. I was really proud. I thought Papa could never fail at anything."

She paused for a moment, and then said:

"They operated on Giorgio in Boston General. He never woke up."

Silvia lowered her head. "My father's been haunted by it ever since. But imagine Mrs. Rizutto. If we hadn't interfered, her son might have lived another six months or even a year. As it is, medical science only made the end quicker."

I was silent for a few seconds and then said gently, "So you decided to become a doctor."

"Not consciously, but I must have carried these feelings with me. Anyway, Sarah's father, a professor of medicine in Cambridge, was the clinical director of a hospice for the terminally ill. One day he let us tag along while he made morning rounds.

"John Conrad was wonderful. I mean, when he spent time with a patient, he made him feel like the most important person in the world. He listened to everyone's worries and somehow found the right words to give each of them courage.

"There was this little boy of eight. Though he was very frail, he still managed a little laugh at the doctor's jokes.

"I suddenly found myself wishing that Giorgio could have died in such a humane and caring place. That day, on the journey back to St. Barts, was when I made up my mind."

"I can imagine your father's reaction."

"Actually, I don't think you can. Though obviously surprised, he seemed to accept my decision. It was only later that he started fighting back. Naturally, he began with guilt."

"That's always a popular one with parents."

"Anyway, when that didn't work, he tried the rigors of a medical education."

"Tell me about it, Doctor," I smiled. "Did he describe the three-day shifts without sleep?"

"In agonizing detail. But I argued that if others had survived it, I could too. And then—bribery. He proposed that we set up something like the Ford Foundation, giving out grants for all sorts of worthy medical causes. I confess to being tempted. But finally, after a summer of fruitless attempts at dissuasion, he surrendered. When he kissed me goodbye he whispered that the most important thing in the world was that I do whatever made me happy."

"Anyway," I said testingly, "isn't it really a question of what you do until you marry Nico?"

"God," she exclaimed with playful annoyance. "You're worse than my father. What makes you so sure I'm in love with him? Did I ever mention that I was?"

"Well, it'd be a great stock merger anyway," I said, avoiding a direct answer.

"I can't deny that much," she conceded.

"Then, have you set a date?" I was suddenly not sure I wanted to hear the answer to that.

"Actually," she said with a mischievous smile, "the fathers recently proposed the last weekend in August."

"You mean this coming August?"

She nodded. "Of course now they'll have to postpone it."

I began to breathe again.

At last I understood the extra dimension of her desire to join Médecine Internationale.

Not only could she work with sick children, but she would be worlds away from Nico Rinaldi and all the familial pressures.

"Tell me, Silvia, did your decision to go to Africa by any chance involve not being able to attend your own wedding?"

She tried unsuccessfully to suppress a grin.

"As a matter of fact, I did explain that I needed time and space to think things over."

"How did they take it?"

"They didn't have a choice. I'm my mother's daughter as well as my father's. She would have asserted all her independence. So now, Mr. Inquiring Reporter, do you have all your answers?"

No, I said to myself. I've just thought of a whole new set of questions.

# EIGHT

AT FIVE O'CLOCK on the last day of our training, François lit a cigarette and made a few heartfelt remarks.

"Okay. We've finished the formal introduction, which, as you'll see the moment you arrive, is no preparation at all. Every day in the field is a learning experience and we can only try to give you a mental attitude that's ready for any possible crisis, which usually turns out to be the one that we didn't prepare you for. I'd just like to say to those of you I've picked on unfairly, I'm sorry. And, to those of you I haven't—don't worry, I'll get to you while we're there."

There was a small ripple of laughter. I think underneath his curmudgeonly exterior there lurked a shy, likable human being.

"Now, good luck, everybody," he concluded,

adding the words I had never expected to hear from him: "I have nothing more to say."

WE WERE SCHEDULED TO LEAVE the next evening and so had three-quarters of a day in Paris to do what we wanted.

Silvia and I went to the Rodin Museum in the morning, then showed up at Médecine Internationale for the last time.

We had various documents to sign, including bank mandates, a health policy in case of medical catastrophe and life insurance for our next of kin. I designated Chaz and my mother each to become five thousand dollars richer in case of my demise.

We then split up for the afternoon to do some shopping for our respective families. I mailed Mom and Malcolm an "antique" ormolu clock as a belated wedding present and some very cute baby clothes from Le Bon Point to my newly pregnant sister-in-law.

On my way back to the hotel, I passed La Voix de Son Maître and went in for a final browse. Naturally, I was incapable of leaving without buying three cassettes, one of which I had gift-wrapped for Silvia.

I PACED NERVOUSLY OUTSIDE THE BUS. It was getting late and we would miss the plane if we didn't get going. I kept glancing at my watch, wondering what the hell might have happened to her.

"Hey, Matthew," François bellowed. "Get on board. Don't worry, she can afford a limo if we leave without her."

I found that neither reassuring nor funny, but I obeyed.

Just as I sat down, Silvia appeared on the top step, followed by her usual shadow.

She looked gorgeous in a loose blue sweater, tight jeans and black leather boots. Flopping down next to me, she patted my hand reassuringly.

"I'm sorry. But they just wouldn't get off the phone."

I thought it best not to ask to whom she was referring.

As we were mired in an automotive swamp at the Place de l'Étoile, François called out, "Take a good look, boys and girls, you'll see more cars from your window right now than in all of Eritrea."

The ever-faithful Nino had the entire back row to himself. When I met his eye, I waved to him cordially to join us. But he stared right past me. He was still on the job and was not about to fraternize.

At Charles de Gaulle, as we threw our luggage onto carts and began to push them toward the gate, her Cerberus still continued to keep watch over his charge from a discreet distance. At last when we reached Passport Control, duties officially ended, he approached Silvia and me. Self-consciously shifting his weight from side to side and mostly looking down at his shoes, he said goodbye.

"I wish Signorina Dalessandro a good journey. I am sorry that I will not be there to look after her. But . . ." He paused, too shy to continue.

"You're a sweetie," she responded warmly. "Thank you for everything. My best wishes to your wife and little girl. *Arrivederci.*"

He glanced at me out of the corner of his eye as if to say, I'm counting on you, mister. Don't screw up. Then he turned and walked slowly down the corridor.

"Are you going to miss him?" I murmured.

"No," she answered categorically.

I took her hand and we hurried to join the others in the Duty Free Shop, making last-minute purchases of essentials like cognac and scotch. Maurice Hermans was struggling to carry a huge two-liter bottle of Dutch geneva.

"Do you know this gin was invented from juniper berries by a Dutch professor of medicine?" he remarked somewhat self-consciously.

"You look like you've got enough to cure all of Eritrea," I said in amusement.

"Well, it was on sale and I thought it might be useful in case the pilot runs out of fuel."

All eleven of us then hung around the departure gate, making small talk and trying not to appear as nervous as we all were.

At last Ethiopian Airlines called flight number 224 to Asmara. François stood at the door of the plane like a drill sergeant, making absolutely sure that every one of his carefully trained medical commandos had made it on board. Naturally he had a tart comment for Maurice's massive bottle of gin. "That thing is grotesque. It's so juvenile of you, Dr. Hermans. The least you could have done is get something respectable like Courvoisier."

He even had criticism for my knapsack, through which a large rectangular package protruded.

"Pray tell, what's that, Dr. Hiller? A Hershey's bar?"

"Sorry to disappoint you, François," I replied. "It's my keyboard. I told you about it."

"Yes," he recalled. "I look forward to not hearing it."

Like broken field runners, Silvia and I shoved and weaved our way down the narrow, crowded aisle to reach our seats.

As we buckled up, she gave me a big smile.

"What was that for?" I asked.

"No reason," she replied. "I'm just *piena di . . . sentimenti.*"

"Full of different feelings." That described my state of mind as well. And I was also unable to translate them all the way.

I reached in my pocket and gave her the box.

"For that new-fangled Japanese tape machine of yours."

"Thank you. Is it 'Hiller's Greatest Hits'?"

"It's a hell of a lot better."

By now she had opened the wrapping and seen that I had bought her selections from Gluck's golden eighteenth-century oldie, *Orfeo ed Euridice.*

"I've never heard it," she confessed.

"Well, it's got the most perfect expression of a lover's longing ever set to music."

She handed me her cassette player. "Find it for me."

Putting on the headset I quickly fast-forwarded to the spot and then returned it to her. She closed her eyes and listened to *"Che farò senza Euridice?"* ("What will I do without Euridice?")

Halfway through she grabbed me by the arm and said, "Matthew, *'che farò senza te?'* What will I do without *you?*"

I leaned over and kissed her. Long. Slow. And sexy.

Suddenly, with a roar, the plane lifted off and soared into the late-evening sky.

I HAD NAIVELY ASSUMED that the flight would provide a temporary respite from our leader's browbeating. But I underestimated his dedication.

As they began to serve the meal, a familiar voice came over the plane's loudspeaker.

"This is Dr. Pelletier speaking. I would like to remind all travelers—especially those in my group—not to forget to take their prophylactic malaria pills. Thank you. *Bon appétit.*"

WE REACHED ASMARA AT ONE O'CLOCK in the morning. All of us were wide-awake with excitement.

I have vivid recollections of my first impressions of Darkest Africa. It was just that—dark. Once our plane landed, the runway lights were extinguished and it was eerie to see the blackness of the airport punctuated only by the glimmer of eyes and teeth.

Customs was perfunctory and we all piled into the back of an asthmatic van. Three other vintage trucks followed with our gear. Silvia fell asleep on my shoulder as our caravan bounced along painfully for nearly two hours.

At last we reached Adi Shuma and the ramshackle compound of rectangular huts with corrugated iron roofs that would be our home for the foreseeable future.

As some of the local staff unloaded our baggage, François called me aside. "Matthew, I'm organizing sleeping quarters and just from a practical standpoint I'd like to know where you plan to spend your nights."

I responded honestly, "Listen, François, I can't answer that now. Can't we just bunk anywhere for the time being?"

He shrugged and walked off, muttering something under his breath about "American puritans."

And so that first night I was billeted with Gilles Nagler, a stocky, earnest-looking Frenchman with wire-rimmed glasses.

We unpacked by candlelight since the primitive gasoline-driven electric generator served only the O.R. and other medical areas.

Gilles noticed my huge package, which I had left wrapped. He was alarmed.

"What's that?" he asked with undisguised concern.

"A piano," I replied.

"No, really, be serious."

"I am serious. It's just a keyboard without the instrument itself."

"Oh, so you mean it will not make any noise?"

"Noise? Perish the thought, Gilles. Anyway what it does make is music, and only in my head."

"Still, I must warn you," he admonished as he withdrew five or six pairs of binoculars from his bag. "I am compulsively neat. I hope you too will keep this place tidy."

"Don't panic. You won't have to keep that close an eye on me. I'm not a closet litterbug." I couldn't help eyeing his collection of optical equipment and he felt obliged to explain.

"In case you were wondering," he offered with some pride, "I am a bird-watcher."

"Of that I have no doubt," I commented and crawled into bed to try and grab a few winks.

"If I'm very lucky I will see the Northern Bald Ibis."

"Sounds wonderful. Goodnight."

I DON'T KNOW HOW LONG I actually slept, but I remember being up with the dawn. Our room was already humid and uncomfortable and getting worse by the minute.

I went to the window to take my first look at Eritrea by daylight and was amazed by what I saw.

"My God," I gasped.

My roommate suddenly woke, groped for his glasses, bounded out of bed and demanded: "What? What's wrong?"

"Nothing," I said. "But I think there might be a big rock concert here tonight."

"Are you insane?"

"Well," I continued to pull his leg, "there's quite a crowd of fans lined up. I can't imagine what else so many people could be waiting for. And Marta seems to be out there distributing programs."

Gilles stared in amazement at the sight of a seemingly endless column of people—emaciated, dusty, obviously unwell—massing from the front door of the clinic to as far back as the eye could see.

"Jesus," he gasped. "Don't they know we don't start till seven?"

"Not all of them have their Rolexes, Gilles. Anyway, I'd say we've got a full day ahead of us."

"Right, Hiller. It looks like Marta's already starting to triage the patients. I must have my two cups of morning coffee. Then we can go and start early."

He was a bit uptight, but obviously dedicated.

As we dressed and shaved quickly (with cold water), Gilles chattered compulsively about birds. How during our "visit," he hoped to catch a glimpse of such winged wonders as the Wattled Crane and—I kid you not—the Brown Booby. He parroted on as we headed to the "refectory," a large (compared to our hut) wooden barnlike structure clearly built in a hurry.

Most of the others were already seated at the long sagging table, including Silvia, who waved that she was saving me a place.

At the far wall was a kitchen of sorts, with a wood-burning stove and some dented steel pots. We had been assured that the native cooks knew basic hygiene and boiled everything twice before serving it. Whether they had been instructed in anything else remained to be seen.

Our breakfast was laid out on a computer: some papaya, bananas and goat cheese to be eaten with *injara,* a kind of rubbery bread roll made of *teff,* a local grain. The coffee urn looked like it had a previous life as a barrel of cooking oil (it had). I sat next to Silvia.

"How do you feel?" I inquired.

"Scared to death. And you?"

"Well, I'd say my dominant mood is impatience. I want to get out there and get started. After all, that's why we're here, isn't it?"

She nodded.

As I wolfed down the food, I looked around at the other faces and sensed in them an urgent energy similar to my own.

Only Silvia seemed subdued.

"Anything wrong?" I asked.

She shook her head. "I've suddenly gone black on the signs and symptoms for schistosomiasis."

"Come on," I put my arm around her shoulder. "You knew it upside down that night in the Café de Flore. You're just getting worked up over nothing. Besides, these diseases flash wildly at you like the neon billboards in Times Square. Believe me, you can't miss them."

She forced herself to smile and then remembered she had not introduced me to the young Tigrean sitting opposite her with whom she had been conversing.

"By the way, Matthew, this is Yohannes. I'm lucky. He's going to be my practical nurse and he speaks the best English of anyone around."

The young man beamed at this high praise. "Surely the doctor is erroneous," he stated. "I am not so extremely linguistic."

From what I'd heard so far, I agreed with him and hoped at least he could translate suitable medical questions to the patients—and especially, transmit the answers.

"Hey," I suddenly noticed. "Where's the great man? Don't tell me he's enjoying a little sleep-in?"

"Are you kidding?" Denise interjected. "François and Maurice have been in the O.R. since we got here last night. There were some badly shot-up guerrillas waiting when we arrived, and they didn't want to risk putting them off till morning."

"Good for them," I said. Then I stood up and, addressing no one in particular, declared, "Let's be duly inspired by their example and go out and bite the bullet" (an unfortunate phrase which revealed my own nervousness).

As we were all about to disperse, Marta called out, "Remember, there's no lunch as such. The food is here, so just come and grab it when you feel you can. Dinner's at seven-thirty and we have a team meeting at nine. Believe me, it's a full day."

"I believe her," I muttered to Silvia as we walked out into the now-blistering morning sun toward the "Patient Consultation Building" (hovel) to which she and Denise had been assigned.

As I kissed her on the forehead, she clutched my hand tightly for a second. "Can I check with you if I need a second opinion?"

"Sure—but you won't."

I puzzled over Silvia's uncharacteristic stage fright for roughly the next two minutes and thirty seconds, approximately the time it took to get to my own richly appointed examination room, throw on a white jacket, wash my hands and diagnose my first case of TB without even having to put on a stethoscope.

This little girl was so patently infected I could hear the lesions on her lungs by the way she breathed.

From then on, I lost track of time.

In the next three hours I saw a more exotic spectrum of diseases than I had in my entire previous clinical experience. I think I encountered every one of the "allegedly extinct" afflictions that Jean-Michel Gottlieb had discussed, including leprosy.

My nurse was a seasoned veteran named Aida. Unlike the famous operatic heroine, she was anything but "celestial."

She was tiny and tough, and I admit that at first I found her bedside manner a bit too aggressive. But I soon realized that she had evolved her technique from years of experience. For the many patients trying to push in front of one another obediently responded to her shouting and occasional shoving.

Also, she helped me begin my study of the Tigrinya language, the first word I learned being the most gratifying for any doctor: *yekanyela*—"thank you."

By the end of the day I could also ask where it hurt, and get some idea of how long the person had been suffering. And when the patient gratefully thanked me, I was able to say "You're welcome."


I WAS KEPT SO CONSTANTLY BUSY that it was only when I stopped to take the obligatory liter of water that I noticed how totally soaked with sweat I was.

For some reason I thought back to my interview in Paris, which now seemed light-years ago, and François's facetious questions about whether I would miss the hedonistic pleasures of civilization like television and McDonald's. In retrospect I realized that he had *not* mentioned anything about air-conditioning.

The only such concession to creature comforts existed in the O.R. (which is perhaps why the canny frog commandeered it).

The clinical areas were scheduled to receive cooling equipment "in the near future." Which, more accurately translated, meant never.

While I savored the free time I had granted myself, I suddenly remembered Silvia.

I left Aida to hold the fort while I took a quick break. I could not bring myself to mention the word "food" because almost all of these patients were on the brink of starvation.

The sun was now at its meridian, a fireball—the beginning of the three-hour period in which the staff had been forbidden to walk out for anything but the shortest distances. And then only if absolutely necessary.

Of course the patients had no alternative but to sit in the burning heat, protecting themselves as best they could with their tattered garments, suffering in silence as they—most of them anyway—obediently waited their turn to be examined by the white-coated medicine men and women from a different world.

Mothers sat motionless, like brown statues nursing their whimpering infants as flies buzzed relentlessly about them. Old people, paper thin, bent with the weight of years, stood mutely by.

Many of them had walked over half a day to get here and were prepared to wait as long as necessary. That meant they would sleep where they stood and receive only water, a token bowl of porridge and the placebo of "better luck next time."

I had only to look at their faces—which I tried not to do—and my heart ached.

When I arrived, Silvia's clinic was utter chaos. Shouting, screaming and pushing. I instantly grasped that for all his eloquence, Yohannes lacked Aida's ability to deal with the physical onslaughts of the more assertive patients.

My attention was immediately seized by the wails and imprecations of a woman in great pain. Then I saw Denise suturing a jagged abdominal laceration on a moaning female patient being held down by volunteers.

"What the hell are you doing?" I asked her. "Can't you give her some more lignocaine?"

"No," she hissed between gritted teeth. "I ran out a few minutes ago."

"Well, I'll get you some," I shouted.

She stared at me, her eyes burning with anger. "There is none, you dumb American bastard. Now leave me alone. Do you think I'm enjoying this?"

"Where's Silvia?" I asked in a chastened tone.

"I don't know, at the beauty parlor probably," Denise snapped. "If you find her, tell her to get her ass back here and pull her weight." Then her tone suddenly changed to a helpless appeal. "*Please,* Matt, I'm reaching my limit."

I could tell she was on the verge of tears. Clearly, for some unfathomable reason, Silvia had deserted. What the hell had happened? I hurried to the refectory and, as I entered, nearly bumped into François.

From the expression on his unshaven face, he was not in a jovial mood. He had obviously just gotten out of the O.R.

"If you're looking for that girlfriend of yours, she's taking the longest coffee break in history," he said with disgust. "I should have known better. But Dalessandro's bribe was too gross to ignore. I guess this is all too much for her pampered sensibilities."

"What are you talking about?"

"She doesn't know, but when she applied, her father offered us a million bucks . . ."

"If you took her?"

"No, *if we turned her down.* That pissed me off so much that I accepted her. Now, if you don't mind, I've got work to do, and so do you."

He stormed out without another word.

I caught sight of Silvia seated at the far end of the table, head propped up on her hand, staring forlornly into a coffee cup. I tried to restrain my anger but I couldn't help feeling disappointed and, yes, embarrassed. For me as well as her.

But then, as I drew near, I reminded myself that since François had surely dressed her down already, the last thing she needed was yet another scolding. She was clearly undergoing a crisis of confidence and needed some support.

"Hi, Silvia," I said quietly. "Wanna talk?"

She shook her head.

"Come on, it'll help if you open up."

She was silent for another moment, then:

"Matthew, I'm so ashamed of myself. All these months I'd been so confident about what I wanted to do. And yet the instant I saw those children my heart just broke and I fell apart."

Oh, so that was it. She had lost her clinical distance. Didn't she realize this was not the time to surrender to such compassionate reactions?

"I should have been tougher," she berated herself.

"If you were tougher, you wouldn't be you," I said softly.

"Well, braver, then. These people live in hell and I can't even face them as an outsider."

"Cut it out," I ordered. "François expected too much on the first day. By the way, have you been drinking regularly?"

She avoided my gaze.

There was no point in castigating her further. I merely went over and brought her two liter bottles of water. "Down one of these now and don't miss another for the rest of the day. And as far as everything else is concerned I have only two words."

"Yes?" She looked at me anxiously.

"Grow up."

For some reason that made her smile.

When we finally left the dining room ten minutes later, she was shored up to face the sternest medical challenges.

Just outside the door she put her arms around me and said, "Thanks, Matthew."

And then she kissed me with a passion that made our embrace on the plane seem like just a friendly peck.


IT WAS NOT AN ORDINARY DAY.

Between dealing with the gunshot wounds of guerrilla fighters, I diagnosed and treated more patients than I could count. Many would have died had we not been there at this moment in their illness.

Moreover our chance arrival prevented blindness in at least a dozen kids with trachoma. This insidious eye infection, always at its worst where hygiene is at its least, would have cost them their sight. But timely dabs of doxycycline (so easy—who can imagine life without antibiotics?) clears the condition entirely.

I will never forget the last trachoma case I saw that day. He was a bright little boy named Dawit who, in his many hours of waiting, had learned one or two words in English. He delighted in addressing me as "dokta" in various tones of voice, giggling after each one. His condition was virulent, but he had not yet begun to scar in the conjunctiva or cornea. A course of doxy would obliterate the condition with no permanent damage.

But we had no more ointment on hand, and I had Aida explain to Dawit's mother that she would have to bring him back the following morning.

The next day mother and son were nowhere to be found.

Neither, it turned out, was a single tube of doxycycline. The moment we restocked, and during the rest of the time I was in Africa, I searched for this little boy to save him from a life of sightlessness. I never found him.

I think the best doctors are the ones who remember their failures as much as their successes. It gives them the necessary humility. That is why when my thoughts turn to Eritrea, I think of those I didn't save. Of little Dawit.

And Silvia.

# NINE

DINNER WAS AS SUBDUED as breakfast had been animated.

Sure, we had been warned a thousand times that this place was deprived. But none of us, not even our battle-hardened leader, had ever seen human beings live in such utter squalor and neglect. I personally wondered how I ever could go out for a simple pizza again, knowing that so many children would spend the nights groaning with hunger in their mothers' arms.

The day had been so hectic that it was difficult to remember back to when Silvia had been a problem. In the afternoon she had steeled herself and become one of us. Her diagnoses were more assured, her manner reassuring. In fact, she made one spectacular call.

Denise was examining a six-year-old child who had been given antibiotics for a chest infection a week earlier in her village by one of the roving UN medical teams. But now, she had been rushed to our clinic, pale, sweaty, with a barely detectable fast thready pulse. When she had difficulty picking up heart sounds from the stethoscope, Denise panicked and called Silvia over to listen.

"Jesus," Silvia reacted instantly. "Get the ultrasound machine in here right away."

"What are you talking about, Dalessandro? This is a viral—"

Silvia cut her off and repeated to the nurse, "Hurry, Yohannes." He dashed off obediently.

"Really," Denise protested. "You haven't got the vaguest idea of what you're doing, have you?"

"Shut up, Lagarde. I think I'm onto something."

In a matter of minutes, Yohannes had returned, wheeling the primitive apparatus we had brought with us. Silvia quickly switched it on and slapped the probe on the child's chest. Her suspicions were immediately confirmed.

"I knew it. She's got a pericardial effusion. Her heart's compressed. No wonder you couldn't hear anything. Are you sure we have no local anesthetic at all?"

"Absolutely."

"Dammit, I'll have to go in there cold."

She commanded Denise to help Yohannes hold the young patient down, trying to bolster her own courage by saying, half aloud, "Come on, Dalessandro, you've got no choice. Just go in and do it fast."

A moment later the child shrieked with pain as she introduced a needle below the breastbone and quickly aspirated some cloudy fluid. In a matter of seconds the compression was relieved and the little girl began to breathe normally.

Silvia bent over, stroked the child's forehead and said gently, "I'm sorry I had to do that. I know it hurt, but there was no other way."

Denise had no alternative. She had to say, "Well done, Dalessandro."

BY THE TIME FRANÇOIS CALLED our flagging group to order that evening, everyone already knew about Silvia's inspired actions.

"I'll make this brief, guys," he began, "because I know you're all dying to sample the swinging local nightlife." We were too bushed to grant him even a token laugh.

"Anyway," he continued, "the only thing we have to discuss tonight is how to make the best use of the few drugs the thieves have left us."

"Did you say 'thieves'?" Maurice asked with astonishment.

"Well, here they're called *shifta,* old boy. But by any other name they're the same black marketeers who, wherever we go, somehow manage to rip off the lion's share of our medications."

"With respect, François—" I began to protest.

"Cut the crap, you mean without respect—"

"Well, without respect, then. If you knew they would try to rob us why didn't you post guards on the vehicles?"

"What the hell do you think I did, Hiller? Unfortunately yesterday the 'guards' themselves drove the whole damn truck away."

Having made me feel like a squashed bug, he now addressed the others.

"We've got to prioritize the surgical procedures very carefully."

Murmurs of discontent grew louder as a handwritten list was circulated among us.

Maurice was livid. "I don't believe this," he stated, slapping the paper for emphasis. "As I see it, we've no lignocaine, no erythromycin and only half the halothane we started with. What can we do, François? Some in-grown toenails?"

I particularly noted that in addition to these major drugs, every tube of ophthalmic antibiotics had disappeared. For the foreseeable future, Dawit and the dozens like him we would diagnose each day would have to go untreated.

"When can we expect some refills?" I inquired with exasperation.

"As soon as our guys in Paris collect the insurance," François answered. "And don't start hassling me about red tape. We're bloody lucky to have insurance at all."

At this moment Silvia raised her hand.

"Yes, Miss FAMA?" His irritation was undisguised.

"May I make a phone call?"

Without waiting for François to reply, the others shouted almost in unison, "No!"

Denise even went as far as to sneer, "Calling for the first flight out, Dalessandro?"

But having spent nearly four solid hours in the heat of battle, Silvia was no longer the lily they had seen wilting at breakfast. Nor did she give a damn about her current standing in the opinion polls.

"I know that I'm not very popular today and I apologize to everyone—especially Denise—for screwing up this morning. However, my request to use the phone was a legitimate attempt to help."

"I'm listening," François said, arms folded.

"I'd like to call my father."

More groans, whistles and boos. Clearly the team had found a scapegoat.

Their smug self-righteousness really pissed me off. I rose and leaned on the table, facing them down one by one.

"All right, you guys, shut up. Let her talk."

The derision subsided and Silvia spoke her piece.

"Being, as all of you know, a filthy capitalist swine, my father's got connections with others of his ilk in the pharmaceutical industry and might be able to expedite the shipment of the drugs we need."

The first response was silence. All eyes fixed on our leader, whose reaction was surprisingly benign.

"Well, as the Ethiopian proverb might go, 'it takes a *shifta* to catch a *shifta*.' So why not give big Daddy a try?"

He reached into his pocket, withdrew a key and handed it to her. "While you're at it, ask him to send a few cases of Chianti Riserva."

Silvia managed to walk straight-backed out of the room, knowing the mockery that would explode in her absence.

"Typical bourgeoise," Denise cracked. "Running to papa for everything."

"Come on, give her a break," I barked. "Considering the esteem in which you already hold her, don't you think it took guts to volunteer her father's influence? Haven't any of you ever had a minute of anxiety or a moment of uncertainty? I still think Silvia's really got the stuff."

"Yes," Marta concurred sarcastically. "It's called money."

Their scornful laughter was interrupted by Silvia's reappearance. Everybody suddenly shut up.

"Thank you," she said quietly to François, handing him back the key. "He knows the guys to call. We can probably expect a stopgap shipment by the end of the week."

"Bravo," my roommate, Gilles, cheered. "Well done, Silvia. By the way, that was a damn good diagnosis this afternoon."

His initiative was followed by some politely grudging applause. It was far from a love feast, but at least the Silvia-bashing was over.

"All right, boys and girls," François proclaimed. "The meeting's finished, everybody get some sleep."

In a matter of seconds Silvia and I were alone, each of us holding a candle. She smiled uneasily.

"Thanks for sticking up for me."

"Thanks for doing what you did. It's going to make a big difference."

She looked beautiful in the flickering light.

"How are things back in Milan?" I asked, trying to sound nonchalant.

"Fine . . . okay."

"How's Nico?"

"I didn't ask."

"Didn't your father tell you?"

"If you want to know the truth, he was happy just talking about me and finding out what you guys were like."

I suddenly wondered about the nature of the report Nino had given. And how much his employer already knew about me.

I decided not to think about it any further. At least at that moment.

"Come on, Silvia, it's getting late. Blow out the candle."

"Why are you looking at me like that?" she asked, as if she could feel my gaze on her cheek.

"Because I want to remember you exactly this way."

Then, without another word, we each extinguished the tiny flames and stood close together in the darkness.

I put my arm around her and switched on my flashlight. We began to walk slowly back to her bungalow.

The compound was totally silent except for the distant cawing of night birds, whose exotic names were known only to the likes of Gilles. The huts and trees were mere shadows against the moon and the temperature was verging on the tolerable.

"Do you know something?" she murmured. "What started as the worst day of my life has ended as the best. And there's a single reason." She squeezed my arm. "How can I ever thank you?"

"It was nothing," I replied.

We were now at her front door. She looked up at me.

"I don't want this day to end."

A moment later we were inside, reaching out for one another by the light of a single candle.

I FIND IT IMPOSSIBLE TO convey what it felt like to touch and kiss Silvia Dalessandro. Or to describe the completeness of my world when we embraced.

Suddenly she stopped. "I have something to tell you, Matthew," she said. "I'm scared. I've never been with a man before."

I was genuinely surprised. I would never have imagined that someone as sophisticated as Silvia was a virgin. But from the expression on her face I could see it was true. Which left me to draw my own conclusions about what I meant to her.

And so we made love for the first time in a small room in a broken-down hut in a remote village in Ethiopia.

# TEN

IT WAS NOT A DREAM.

I awoke in what seemed the middle of the night and found that I was still next to Silvia. That she was breathing peacefully in my arms. I could scarcely believe it. She looked more beautiful than ever. I wanted to kiss her and yet could not disturb her slumber.

I looked at my watch: it was after five. Through the makeshift shutter of her window, I could now see filaments of daylight beginning to radiate in the darkened sky. I had to get back.

Though I dressed as quietly as I could, she suddenly opened her eyes, sat up on her elbow and looked at me in the chiaroscuro of the new morning.

At first she simply stared and then said, "No."

"No what?"

"You can't leave, Matthew."

I leaned my cheek close to hers. "Do you want them to find out?"

"What does it matter? They'll see it on my face, anyway."

"Yes," I smiled. "Can you see it on mine?"

She nodded. "So you can stay."

"No," I joked. "I don't want to make Gilles jealous."

As she laughed I broke free of her spell and forced myself to do what I knew was the right thing.

"Matthew—"

I stopped and whispered, "Don't worry, we're just starting a whole new chapter. See you later."

GILLES STIRRED AS I ENTERED OUR HUT. He reached quickly for his glasses, but I reassured him,

"Don't sweat, it's early. I just went for a little walk."

"Oh, yes, of course," he answered in a tone I couldn't decipher. "And don't worry, you didn't disturb me. I've been training myself to wake at five to watch the birds. Since you are up, do you want to come along?"

I thanked him for his generosity and promised I would go another time. Meanwhile I was grateful that he was either oblivious to what was going on, or generous enough to act it. In any case, I hoped he would spot the bluebird of happiness this morning.

OUR CHARADE CONTINUED for the better part of forty-eight hours. My teammates did not seem to notice any change in our behavior and we were happy for the privacy.

And then, on the third morning, François dispatched the two of us in the half-track to attend to an ailing chieftain. I should have suspected his magnanimity in allowing me to take a friend on what should otherwise have been an easy one-man house call.

When we returned, he was grinning broadly.

"Guys, I've had to relocate you. From now on you're both living in hut eleven. That's if you don't mind . . ."

Silvia and I exchanged glances.

"No," I answered on our behalf. "We'll force ourselves."

Then I realized, "Hey, there are only ten huts."

"Well, believe it or not, Hiller, we've already moved your stuff to the compound's latest residential development."

"Do you mean mine too?" Silvia asked with amused astonishment.

"No, we thought you'd prefer to do it yourself. After clinic hours, of course. Anyway, some of our convalescing patients from the EPLF are terrific with their hands. They put the whole thing up in record time while you were away this morning."

It certainly looked it. The structure was in its way an architectural classic, combining the rectangularity of a telephone booth and the gentle sloping of the Tower of Pisa. But what the hell, it had the inestimable advantage of being on the far side of the storehouse, apart from the others, and however humble, it was our first home. Silvia and I stood hand in hand, looking at the freshly built abode.

"Happy?" I asked.

She smiled. "I told you everyone would tell."

"That's good. It saves us the trouble of telling everyone."

At that moment François called from afar.

"May I remind you two that this is not an excuse to be even a minute late for your afternoon duties."

Needless to say, our nights were memorable.

And we were very happy.

YET, IN THE MERCILESS HEAT of the day, we could not be oblivious to our surroundings.

The earth was parched. Except for the defiantly bold violet flowers of the jacaranda trees, nothing seemed to blossom or grow. The landscape was oppressively monochrome—dull brown with a barely perceptible tinge of red. In moments of reflection I sometimes fantasized that this was the result of all the blood that killing ground had absorbed.

From our clinic, we could hear the occasional tattoo of gunfire. It was a troubling sound, not least because it signaled the imminent arrival of its victims for surgery. Naturally I did not ask my wounded patients' political affiliation. Some of them were so young I was not always sure if they knew themselves. Which only reemphasized the mindlessness of war.

Silvia's father could really make things happen. Before the first week ended, helicopters from his oil exploration on the Dahlak islands were ferrying new shipments of drugs from the Asmara airport safely to our backyard. The patients thronging nearby cheered and broke into a welcome dance for the magic-bearing whirlybirds.

We, on the other hand, celebrated by performing surgery. And giving doxycycline to the sufferers of trachoma (alas, not Dawit).

Only the tempo at which we worked made it tolerable. There was simply no time to feel horrified by the dreadful diseases we encountered. It is one thing to see an illustration in a book but it is quite another to confront the condition *in vivo* on the grossly disfigured face of an otherwise cherubic child.

EXCEPT FOR OUR MEDICAL DUTIES, Silvia and I spent every waking moment together. For the others, the exhausting sameness of each day inevitably wore them down. For us, it was an endless repetition of pure happiness. Yet, the unacceptable losses we sustained each day eventually took their toll even on us.

I could exorcise my own pain by practicing on the dummy piano. But Silvia had no such outlet and needed to talk about her own feelings. I could tell without her saying a word when things had been particularly difficult and she needed consolation.

She would come home, change into her bathrobe and hurry to the makeshift outdoor showers which, if you timed it well, would still be tepid from the heat of the day.

When she returned she would sit on the bed close to me as I played feverishly, the instrument stretched out across my knees. Without music there was no way she could tell what piece I was working on, so I explained:

"It's the *last* movement of Beethoven's so-called 'Moonlight Sonata.' Whoever gave it that stupid title never heard this part—it's really wild. Ludwig really unleashes a whirlwind."

Then I plunged back into the frenzied arpeggios and crashing chords with all the force in my body.

"You're an incredible artist," she said, kissing the back of my neck. "I look at your face and see such total involvement." She smiled. "I sometimes hear the music too."

Then I would stop and we would talk about our day. Because we had to. That is the only way we could preserve our sanity.

SILVIA HAD A TENDENCY to blame herself when she lost a patient. When she had attended the stillbirth of twins early one afternoon, she spent the better part of the evening castigating herself.

It took all my powers of persuasion to convince her that the antenatal care in this country was not merely poor but nonexistent. Indeed, many of the expectant mothers walking miles to the clinic lost their babies before they even reached us. She was quiet for a moment, and then said solemnly under her breath, "Sometimes I hate this place."

"No, you don't," I countered, taking her into my arms.

SINCE THE REFECTORY WAS THE ONLY "recreational" building with electricity, we all hung around there after dinner, reading week-old newspapers, writing letters, talking shop or—yes—smoking. The stress was really brutal and one or two of us had relapsed into old habits.

Often we would try to catch the news on the BBC World Service on the shortwave radio. We listened avidly, especially when they mentioned the Eritrean rebels' fight for independence from Ethiopia. They seemed to know more in London about what was happening on our doorstep than we did.

The other doctors had no social life to speak of. Gilles's birds were of course the winged kind. Most of the time he sat alone reading or brooding. And yet he did not seem to enjoy his own company. I tried to get him to join the rest of us. He was reluctant.

"These conversations always degenerate into talking about one's personal history," he commented dourly.

"So what? That might be interesting."

"Not me. I have no personal history."

The Good Samaritan in me persisted.

"You can always make up the details. I'm sure most of the others do."

"I have no imagination either."

At that point I had used up my supply of pastoral generosity.

Thus, when the last readers had exchanged the last paperbacks, there was nothing left to while away the hours till bed but gossip.

Gradually we learned each other's life stories, the various adventures and misadventures that brought us together in this oasis of boredom. Inevitably the backgrounds of our colleagues became our principal entertainment.

I guess it was predictable that François was the first to open up. That he was married we knew from the ring on his left hand. That it was not the most heavenly union we could deduce from Madame Pelletier's eternal absence—even from the airport when we left.

One evening he inspired some lively debate on the subject of matrimony by referring to himself in passing as a "happily married man." I could not suppress an involuntary, "Really?"

"Really, Hiller," he affirmed. "We've been together for twenty years and have three interesting children."

"How much time do you spend with them?"

"Such things should not be measured by quantities, old boy."

"I know, I know, but judging from the time you've spent overseas, your brief family experiences must be spectacularly intense."

At this point Maurice Hermans asked the question we had all been dying to pose.

"If I may be so bold, François, what does your wife get out of this arrangement?"

"Well," he began slowly, lighting a cigarette, "she's married without the inconvenience of having a husband always underfoot. Of course she's proud of the work I do. She herself is a director of our fund-raising office and she's a good mother."

So far no score, I thought to myself. But there was more.

"Every August, at our cottage in Normandy, we remind ourselves that sex is like fine champagne—when it sparkles at the beginning, it's even better twenty years later. And we fill our fleeting togetherness with such civilized conversation, we momentarily forget that we no longer love each other."

Needless to say there were no further questions.

AS TIME PASSED, PHRASES LIKE "when I'm back in Paris" began to creep into everyday conversation. Now and then we all had to remind ourselves of the idealism that had originally brought us to this distant troubled place. For we were gradually turning into characters from Sartre's *No Exit*. Only, instead of hell being "other people," it turned out to be the *same people*.

At the beginning of our odyssey when Maurice Hermans played his harmonica, he showed us all the courtesy of sitting on the porch when he felt musical. But with the passage of time, he not only moved his performances indoors, but even began to compete with the BBC.

In principle even this would have been tolerable. Unfortunately his repertory consisted only of "Red River Valley" and "My Darling Clementine." There were vague whispers of a lynching party.

ONE NIGHT IN EARLY MAY we heard on the radio that Aldo Moro, former Premier of Italy, had been found murdered by left-wing terrorists. Silvia was shaken. Not only did it bring back shuddering memories of her own mother's fate, but Moro had been a personal friend of her father's.

I tried to comfort her. "At least you're safe from that sort of thing here." I made her promise not to listen to the news again. "Might as well take advantage of being in the middle of nowhere. We have enough to worry about with our patients."

She nodded and clasped my hand. "You're right, we should treasure these moments." For me these words had a penumbra of sadness. They served to remind me that the idyll could not last forever.

Once in a while I dared to ponder about the future. But it seemed so fraught with pain that I couldn't bear even thinking about the inevitable separation that lay ahead of us.

And yet despite the efforts of my rational mind, I did fantasize about marrying Silvia. One night I performed an emergency Caesarean section to help one of the midwives who was in trouble with a breech delivery. As I wrapped the baby up in a blanket and handed it to its mother, I succeeded in conjuring up the face of a child Silvia and I might make together. It was an ephemeral moment of unadulterated joy after which my imagination failed me.

There was no way I could envisage a life in the real world where we would be together. I mean, would she come back to Dearborn with me and practice medicine? Not likely. Would I go to Italy? Not very plausible either. I couldn't see myself being welcomed into her Milanese social circles.

I began to believe that we were the playthings of a cruel destiny that brought us together only to cause us the greater pain of tearing us apart. Inevitably I could not keep these thoughts from Silvia, who readily confessed that her own mind was besieged by the same specter of separation.

"I mean, we're so happy now," I insisted. "Why can't we just go on living like this forever?"

"I agree."

At first I could not believe I had heard her correctly.

"Everything's perfect now," she reasoned. "Why can't we stay here in Africa? There's a lifetime of work to do."

"Are you serious, Silvia? You mean you'd actually give up all the other things in your world?"

"Love and work are all that matter, Matthew. My world begins and ends right here."

"Well, I'd like to share my life with you, if you're sure that's what you really want."

"That *is* what I really want."

"Then will you marry me?"

"I have three words to say to that: *Yes, yes* and *yes.*" Her dark eyes shining, she flung her arms around me.

"Why don't we go and see a priest?"

"That's okay with me." It didn't matter how we got married as long as we did.

I volunteered to phone the Catholic Cathedral in Asmara and make an appointment for us. When did she want to go?

"The sooner the better," she replied.

Then it occurred to me. "I mean, you aren't pregnant by any chance, are you?"

"No, but the idea suddenly appeals to me." Then in a more serious tone of voice, she allowed:

"Actually, to be honest, now that we've decided, I'd be happier if we could present my father with a fait accompli. I can't explain it, it's just my instinct."

I knew she was right. The longer we waited, the more likely it would be that somehow word would reach this very powerful man who could move heaven and earth—and certainly Eritrea—to pluck his daughter away from me.

Without saying why, we asked François for a long-overdue furlough so we could go to Asmara.

"Of course," he agreed good-naturedly. "And be sure to try the restaurant on the sixth floor of the Nyala Hotel. The tables are laid out like little tents. Their *zigini* is quite amusing."

TWO DAYS LATER WE STARTED OUT from Adi Shuma at seven A.M., and well before noon we were at the outskirts of the capital of Eritrea, a full mile higher in altitude. The change in weather was dramatic: we had left the inferno of summer behind and driven into spring.

As we entered the city, we experienced a cultural shock. After so much time in the barren African wilderness, we suddenly came upon what looked like a suburb of Milan. And not without reason. The majority of the architecture dated back to the Italian conquest of the city in 1889, after which this became the seat of Italy's African empire.

Asmara, the "Forest of Flowers," lived up to its name, with bougainvillea and jacaranda everywhere. The streets were immaculate, with outdoor cafés and real shops instead of market-day merchandise on blankets. Yet even here, our beat-up half-track did not look out of place. Nearly half the traffic was horse-drawn.

Since we were not there as sightseers, we headed straight down Liberty Avenue and parked near the Catholic Cathedral, a huge Italianate structure that dominated its surroundings. With a few minutes to kill, we strolled around the interior, looking at the twentieth-century stained-glass windows pretending to be gothic masterpieces.

I was suddenly sidetracked by something wonderful, my weeks of longing unexpectedly fulfilled. And without stopping to ask permission, I found myself quickly pulling out the stops of the cathedral organ. I had not played in many weeks.

Naturally it would have to be Bach's great Fugue in G Minor, and the first measures were halfway to heaven when a loud voice shouted over the powerful music.

"May I ask who you are?" it demanded.

I was so elated to be playing again that my answer may have been slightly disrespectful.

"Right now I'm nothing but a humble servant of J. S. Bach. We've got an appointment with Vicar General Yifter. Do you know where we find him?"

"You have," the man replied. "You are early, my children." Adding magniloquently, "You have obviously flown here on the wings of love."

Like most of his countrymen, Monsignor Yifter was compactly built, although considerably better upholstered than the people around Adi Shuma. He was balding and slightly jowly, with wire glasses pressed tightly against his face, giving him a look of sharp intelligence. He had been staring at me pointedly for some time, assuming I would get his message, until finally he was obliged to say, "That will be quite enough of the music, Mr. Hiller. Will you both come this way?"

Coffee for three was waiting in his book-lined office. I could not help but notice the proliferation of Latin texts.

"Please," he said, motioning to the refreshment, "the beans are grown locally by some of our Capuchin brethren."

"Ah," I could not resist the remark, "then it's *real* caffè cappuccino."

He gave me an odd look and then what I assumed was his best attempt at a smile.

"So, my children, you are very far from home. Did you meet here in Africa?"

"No, Monsignor, three months ago in Paris while we were training for the trip."

"Ah," the cleric remarked, "then you haven't known each other long?"

Was I imagining things or did I sense an edge of suspicion in his question?

"I suppose in bare chronological terms it's a short time," I answered on our behalf. "But we've been living together—by that I mean working night and day—ever since. In those circumstances you can really get close to a person."

"Ah, yes," Monsignor Yifter allowed. "News of your good work has reached us even here. You are to be congratulated. Now, where shall we begin?"

Well, I thought to myself, you can start by acting a little friendlier. I could imagine that his off-the-street trade was not so heavy that he could afford to turn away possible converts like myself.

He leaned back in his chair, pressing the fingers of both hands together, and looked at Silvia.

"Marriage is a very serious undertaking, Miss Dalessandro. And it is of course an eternal and unbreakable bond."

Silvia glanced at me. My expression revealed growing impatience with his patronizing manner.

She turned and said in a conciliatory tone, "We understand that, Monsignor. That's why we've come to put ourselves in your hands. I attended St. Bartholomew's in Wiltshire."

He seemed to like the sound of that and addressed his reply directly to Silvia.

"Quite."

What the hell did that mean?

Silvia now pressed him. "Then, will you marry us?"

"Of course, of course, all in the fullness of time. But it is a practice of the Church to prepare couples for matrimony with a series of some five or six visits. Are you prepared to meet on a monthly basis?"

I wasn't sure, but I think he had just postponed our wedding by half a year. I was wrong.

"Of course, in this case," he appended, "we have a non-Catholic partner." He then looked at me.

"Do I understand you are willing to take instruction?"

"Yes. And do I understand that I don't have to formally convert if I decide not to?"

"Yes, as long as you agree to raise the children in the true faith."

For a split second I did not react. I had already told Silvia that I was willing to have Catholic children, but I did not like this guy putting me under pressure. Still, I knew there was only one word that would get us out of there, so I said it: "Yes."

"Excellent." His reaction was the most enthusiastic of the day. "I'm sure for someone of your education that would not involve more than an additional three months."

No, it was now a nine-month delaying tactic.

I merely nodded.

"Splendid." He rose to his feet. "Then, is this time of day convenient for you?"

"Yes, Monsignor," Silvia said politely. "That means we can make it here and back in a single day."

"Very well, shall we meet in . . ." He reached into the pocket of his robes and withdrew a neat leather diary. Leafing through the pages studiously, he then proposed, "Shall we meet again on the twenty-fourth?"

That was three weeks away.

"Fine," Silvia answered for us both and with that grabbed me by the arm and pulled me out.

The moment we were beyond earshot she whispered, "Deep breaths, Matthew. Take deep breaths. Wait 'till we're in the street."

To reach the car we had to return through the cathedral porch.

It was only then that the bronze plaque on the back wall caught our eye. It was dated 1922 and commemorated the original benefactors of the church. They included none other than Vincenzo Dalessandro, founder of the FAMA Corporation, and the friend he served so faithfully, Il Duce, Benito Mussolini.

"Well, that explains a lot," I remarked sarcastically. "Did you know this was a family chapel?"

"If I had, do you think I would have suggested it?"

She then looked at me with those beautiful eyes and asked tenderly, "Do you still want to marry me?"

"Of course, Silvia. Any place but here."


OUR EXPERIENCES AT THE ITALIAN and American embassies were the polar opposite. The affable local functionaries promised to do everything they could to expedite their respective governmental permissions to marry abroad. They both assured us that we could schedule the event for two weeks' time.

At the risk of disappointing François, we canceled our reservation for that evening at the Nyala Hotel and had a quick espresso in the Café Park before setting off home.

"What are you thinking, Matthew?" Silvia asked.

"Just wondering," I said.

"About what?"

"About how long it's going to take your father to bust us up."

She grabbed my hand. "Don't be silly. Nothing could ever separate us."

"Don't be too sure."

"Come on, be realistic. We're over twenty-one. How could he stop us?"

"Silvia," I said, only half-joking, "with your father's connections he could send you on the first Italian space mission to Mars."

WE GOT HOME LATE THAT NIGHT but were so happy to be in familiar surroundings that we made passionate love for hours.

Afterwards we lay there quietly, in each other's arms.

Silvia whispered, "Matthew, it doesn't make any difference."

"What?"

"We already are married."

I held her tight. Nothing else mattered, really.

# ELEVEN

"NO, FRANÇOIS, you can't make me do this."

If this had been the army I would have been court-martialed for disobedience.

When I committed myself to this mission I thought that there was no task too odious or disturbing that I could not perform, but I was wrong. I discovered that I was incapable of aiming a weapon at another human being and pulling the trigger. Ironically, it was François of all people who was testing my pacifism.

"Look, Matthew, be realistic. There's a war going on barely a hundred meters outside these gates. You may find yourself having to protect your patients' safety. You owe it to them as well as to yourself to know how to use this firearm."

Yet body language betrayed his real feelings: I could tell from the squeamish manner in which he dangled the .38 caliber automatic pistol from his fingers that he too was repelled at holding an instrument of death in a hand trained to save life. "I'll tell you what—to assuage your guilt, I propose the following compromise: learn to use this thing, and defer the decision about actually firing till the problem stares you straight in the face."

He stopped, took an exasperated breath and added, "At least promise me that you'll acquire the option."

I surrendered.

At 6:30 A.M. for the next two weeks we all gathered in a remote corner of the compound, as far as possible from the throng of patients who daily lined up well before we opened our doors.

François displayed a hitherto hidden artistic flair—constructing three cardboard people with half a dozen concentric circles pasted on their hearts. He then placed "Harpo," "Chico" and "Groucho" at distances of ten, twenty and thirty meters respectively and showed us how to dispatch them with merciless accuracy. Some of my fellow doctors, including Silvia, enjoyed the exercise. And yet, irony of ironies, I proved to be the best shot among us. Even François was impressed.

"If you ever get tired of curing people, Hiller, you could always be a Mafia hit man," he joked. Needless to say I did not laugh.

François's gun quickly achieved talismanic status. It became our Excalibur: It would protect us from all evil and allow us to perform our hieratic duties unharmed.

We had arrived in 1978, just as the civil war had reached a new and dangerous phase. The ever-adventurous Soviets had intruded upon the scene, massively re-arming the Ethiopian regime. Their vastly increased firepower turned the tide against the Eritrean rebels and wrought bloody havoc everywhere as they retreated.

These setbacks displaced masses of people and UN Relief workers were frantically setting up refugee camps. The latest one in our area some forty miles east of Kamchiwa had merely two nurses, first-aid equipment and some "holding" staples like dioralyte for the inevitable dysenteries that took such a toll, especially on the children. Since we were the closest equivalent of a "hospital," we regularly sent out a pair of doctors to treat the more urgent cases among these refugees.

Though it did not seem reckless at the time, Silvia and I looked forward to making these trips together. For us it combined the simultaneous opportunity to display altruism and enjoy intimacy, enabling us to win "brownie points" and enjoy each other's company for hours on the road.

And yet we were aware that the journey was not without its perils. Ethiopian troops, ELA rebels and just plain *shifta* fought, like rival urban gangs, regular and pointless battles for turf, heedless of who got caught in their crossfire.

We were about to leave for our third trip to Kamchiwa. In the final moments of preparation, François and Marta helped us check the supplies we had loaded into the back of our well-worn half-track. Without comment François removed the pistol from the glove compartment and checked that it was loaded.

As he kissed Silvia goodbye, I begged him to spare me the same display of affection. Not that I didn't love him, but I couldn't stand the smell of his Gauloises any closer than necessary.

As one would expect from the heiress apparent of FAMA, Silvia drove with panache. If I had let her, she would have kept the wheel the entire way. The early-morning weather was temperate, and driving vaguely resembled a pleasure.

I was relegated to map-reader and disc jockey (for my first cassette I chose Telemann's trumpet concerti to reflect the mood and optimism of a new day). And then luxuriating in the pleasure of being on our own, we talked.

We began by playing yet another round of a game we had invented: Who would be most pissed-off at not being invited to our wedding? That got us through a few bumpy miles, at which point we discussed another hardy perennial: how long we would stay after our two-year contract expired.

"Well, as far as I'm concerned," I said affectionately, "forever doesn't seem long enough. What's the matter, Silvia, got a sudden pang of homesickness?"

"Whatever for?"

"I don't know, a really good bowl of pasta, maybe."

She seemed to blush slightly as she replied, "Don't worry, Matthew, I swear to you I'll learn to cook."

"Come on, you know I wasn't serious about your culinary skills. On the other hand, when it comes to having kids . . ."

"You mean, where do we want to bring them up?"

"Yes," I replied, withholding the full depth of my sudden yearning for paternity. Neither of us had an easy answer for that.

We rode on for a bit, letting Renata Scotto and Placido Domingo serenade the wilderness with the strains of *Tosca*. Silvia seemed pensive.

"A *birr* for your thoughts, Signorina."

"D'you think we'll ever go back?"

"Where?"

"You know, where we came from?"

"Yeah, for our first grandchild's wedding."

She smiled.

By the time we had driven for two hours, Glenn Gould was playing (too fast, in my opinion) Bach's *Goldberg Variations,* and the air was already an oven. When we reached a cluster of eucalyptus trees, I made Silvia pull over. We both drank tea with honey (part of Mother François's recipe for washing down salt tablets and keeping heat stroke away) and then I took over the Graham Hill duties.

A few minutes later the road opened out onto a broad expanse of high ground. We were already forewarned that this topography was the most dangerous, since potential aggressors could see us without being seen. But then, we were young and in love and who the hell would want to hurt us, anyway?

A moment later we found out. At first it sounded like a piece of gravel. In the middle of the African nowhere? Obviously I was unwilling to believe that what had pierced the right side of the hood was a bullet. But then with a huge hiss the steam from the punctured radiator began to spray out. It was all I could do to keep control of the vehicle and bring it to a halt. I remember my eloquent appraisal of the situation at that moment: "Shit!"

"What is it?" Silvia asked, suddenly frightened.

"Not what," I corrected her, "*who.* I wonder if my AAA card is good out here." Gallows humor.

I could feel the veins in my forehead pounding as I reached into the glove compartment, grabbed the pistol and clambered out to see what was going on. At that moment I came face to face with our antagonists: two wiry mahogany-skinned fighters with bandoleers crisscrossed on their chests. They were full of menace, holding what even I recognized as Russian rifles waist high, pointed directly at us.

Ever the intellectual, I attempted to engage them in discourse.

"What do you guys want?" I growled in my best Tigrinya. My heart was pumping so loud against my ribs that I was afraid I would not hear their answer.

They were taken aback for a second by a gringo speaking their own language. The taller of the two eyed me sulphurously. Incongruously, we could still hear Glenn Gould playing in the background.

"You come with us," he barked. There was no way on earth that I would let Silvia be taken by these characters. It would literally have to be over my dead body.

"Get the hell out of our way," I yelled back, adding some choice curse words I had learned from hearing our patients in great pain. The rich vernacular momentarily stymied them again. I called back to Silvia to get into the driver's seat quickly and let me know the instant she was ready to shift gears.

She was obviously in shock. "No, Matthew, maybe we should do what they say."

"Listen to me, dammit," I snapped, trying to rouse her from paralysis. "You don't want to be their prisoner. Now, do what I told you!"

At this point one of the ambushers motioned me with his rifle to come toward him. I refused to move, although I knew he was about to pull the trigger.

"Hurry, Silvia!" I shouted again. There was still no reaction from inside the half-track.

The man's eyes blazed with anger and his intentions were clearly homicidal. At that moment I became a creature of instinct—an animal who would protect his mate at any cost.

A bullet suddenly whizzed past my ear, cutting my final link with civilization. In a furious rage I aimed my gun and fired straight at his chest. I came perilously close to hitting him as he dropped to his knees to avoid the shot. Before he could scramble to his feet again, I had jumped onto the running board. Suddenly I spied a third gunman on the other side of the road. He was lifting his rifle to his shoulder, aiming straight at Silvia.

Instinctively, without hesitation, I fired. He recoiled backwards. My God, I had just shot a man. It was the most horrifying moment of my life and yet I had no time to think twice about it. I quickly reached over, shook Silvia and shouted her name at the top of my lungs. This startled her into awareness. She suddenly came alive, shifted gears and we took off in a cloud of dust.

But by now there was a hail of bullets coming from both sides. As we slowly gained momentum, I reached out of my window and emptied my pistol at the enemy. All hell had broken loose. The air was exploding with imminent death.

In the next instant I felt something tear at my temple. The inside of my head was suddenly flashing like the Fourth of July.

Then everything went black.

PART TWO

# SUMMER
# 1978

#  TWELVE

A GENTLE SUNLIGHT was streaming through the windows, caressing my face as I slowly regained consciousness. I gradually became aware that I was in some sort of hospital bed. My skull ached; there was a drip in my arm. Standing above me, her face tired and careworn, was my mother. What was she doing here? Where was I?

Mom looked enormously relieved that I had opened my eyes.

"Matthew, can you understand me?" she asked apprehensively.

Though scarcely awake, my instant reaction was: *"Where's Silvia?"*

I tried desperately to speak, gulping the air, but unable to create the sounds.

I felt a hand touch mine affectionately and heard the sound of my brother's voice:

"Take it easy, Matthew," he said. "You've been through a helluva lot. I mean, you'll actually be able to boast to your grandchildren that you got shot in the head and lived to tell the tale."

At last I managed to get the words out.

"Chaz, is she all right? Did she get away?"

He seemed not to understand my question and simply answered soothingly, "Try to relax. The main thing is that you're okay."

"No, it's not," I protested, growing more and more agitated.

A stocky, gray-haired man in a white coat came into my field of vision, preempting the conversation. He spoke in strangely accented English.

"Dr. Hiller, do you know where you are?"

At this point I wasn't even sure *who* I was.

Again in this odd accent, the gentleman politely explained, "You are at the *Universitätsspital*—University Hospital, Zurich."

Switzerland! The news did not make my mind any clearer. What was I doing here?

"My name is Professor Tammuz. Five days ago we admitted you with a bullet lodged in the sphenoid bone, very close to the brain. The situation was quite serious. I operated immediately and I am pleased to see that you are back with us."

My mother explained further, "Malcolm flew over with us last week, and was right at Professor Tammuz's shoulder during the whole procedure. He said it was a superb job. Unfortunately he had urgent patients of his own and had to rush back to Dearborn."

My head was groggy, but what I was hearing was doing nothing to make things any more coherent.

"How the hell did I get here?"

"Apparently you were flown in a private air ambulance," Chaz volunteered.

I looked desperately at the professor. "Who else was with me?"

"A young neurologist and a nurse."

"Wasn't there an Italian girl?" My eyes were imploring him. "I mean, there had to be. Silvia was with me, I know she was. She's beautiful, dark-haired, about five foot ten."

"I'm afraid there was no one else on the plane," Tammuz repeated with surgical finality.

I must have been very drugged, because I was having trouble communicating to my family the urgency of it all. At this moment I still did not even know if Silvia was alive. The very thought made my soul ache.

"Chaz," I looked up at my brother, "how did you find out where I was?"

"We got a call from a doctor in Milan. He wasn't very prodigal with details. He simply told us that you'd been injured and were being flown to Zurich to be operated on by the best neurosurgeon in the world. From what I've seen, everything he said was right."

At this point the professor intervened again.

"Can you remember anything that happened before the bullet?" he asked.

I tried to think. Yet the mental effort to recollect the most recent events was indescribably difficult. Despite the discomfort, I tried to assail the fortress of my memory and breach its stone walls.

"There were these two guys—three. With rifles. They tried to take us prisoner. They opened fire. I shot back. I think I hit one of them." Even at this moment I could not confront the possibility that I had actually killed another human being. I was more concerned about the woman I loved, so I shouted to no one in particular:

"Silvia Dalessandro was with me when we were attacked. Will someone please tell me what happened to her?"

My mother answered, herself betraying a sense of worry.

"Matthew, we don't know any more than the doctor's told you. Back home there was a small item on the news wires. It said that an American volunteer had been shot in Eritrea. There was no mention of any other victim."

To which my brother added:

"Surely for someone that well-known there would have been a headline 'Heiress Kidnapped' or something?"

I was at my wits' end. "This can't be possible," I exploded. "She can't have just disappeared."

My desperation was contagious. My family grew increasingly concerned about my own well-being. Each of them tried to find a way to calm me down.

"Maybe Dr. Pelletier knows something," Chaz offered. "Actually, he phoned yesterday and we promised to inform him the moment you woke up."

"Good idea," I agreed eagerly. "Let's try him right away."

It took nearly two hours to get through to Eritrea, but at last I heard François's voice sounding like he was speaking through a mattress of static.

"Welcome to consciousness, Matthew. I'm glad that you're back with us again. I admire your bravery, but whatever possessed you to indulge in such cheap heroism?"

"Cut the crap, will you? Is Silvia alive or dead?"

He hesitated for a split second and then said tonelessly, "Alive, of course, thanks to you. She was the one who brought you back."

"Then where is she?"

"I honestly don't know. And that's the truth, Matthew."

Thank God, I thought to myself, the woman I was going to marry was alive and safe. But why wasn't she here with me?

"Who arranged for the air transport?" I demanded.

"Uh, I did," he answered. Even in my semicomatose state I could feel he was hiding something.

"And where did Silvia go?"

"I assumed she was with you in Zurich. The last thing I saw she was holding your hand as they lifted you into the helicopter."

"What helicopter?"

"One of those Italian choppers from the Red Sea Oil Rig that helped us move the drugs from the airport. Remember? It picked you up and she went along. I mean, man, you saved her life!"

"François, do you have her phone number in Milan?"

"Yes. But I doubt it will do you much good."

What did he know that he wasn't saying?

"Give it to me anyway."

I handed the phone to Chaz, who jotted down the series of digits François gave him. I then said a quick goodbye and ordered my brother to get me the number right away.

A man with a deep voice answered. "May I speak to Silvia Dalessandro?" I asked politely in Italian.

"I'm sorry, sir," he replied laconically.

Dammit, I couldn't even wring out of him whether Silvia was there or not. As a last resort, I decided to go for broke.

"May I speak to Mr. Dalessandro, please?"

"*Prego?*"

"Look, don't play stupid. Put your boss on. This is about his daughter—the one whose life I saved."

Somehow this made an impression. He put me on hold. A few moments later a gentleman who spoke English with the patina of a BBC announcer picked up the phone.

"Good evening, Dr. Hiller. Dalessandro here. I can't thank you enough for what you did. And I'm delighted to hear you're better. I was most concerned until I heard the latest prognosis."

Jesus. You mean, the guy was actually monitoring my condition and never thought to call me and thank me? Something instinctively told me my time would be very short, so I blasted to the point.

"Where's Silvia?"

His riposte—for it really was not an answer—was as smooth as silk. "She was very upset, Matthew. I'm sure you can understand that."

"Can I speak to her?"

"I don't think this is the moment."

What a patronizing bastard.

"Well, when the hell do you think the 'moment' will be?"

"I think it's best that we not continue this conversation," he answered politely but firmly. "Goodbye, Doctor."

I had a strong premonition that this was to be my last communication with the Dalessandro family, so I was determined to hang on tenaciously and get everything in. "Goddammit, Mr. Dalessandro, don't you realize I probably killed a man for her?"

Not even this wild outburst moved him. He replied with unruffled composure—and apparently deep sincerity.

"Matthew, I'll always be grateful to you for saving my daughter's life."

And then he hung up.

I fell back on my pillow in total agony.

And wished that the bullet that pierced my skull had gone all the way.

# THIRTEEN

## In Italy, The "Royal Marriage" That Unites Two Dynasties

MILAN, August 4th 1978 — The closest thing to a royal wedding modern Italy will ever see took place in Milan today. It united that country's most eligible bachelor, Niccolo Rinaldi, 41, son and heir of the Chairman of the multinational METRO corporation, and Dr. Silvia Dalessandro, aged 25, daughter of the Director of the still-bigger conglomerate FAMA.

Observers are already predicting that this will inevitably lead to the biggest corporate merger in the history of Italian industry.

The ceremony was private and attended only by the immediate families.

The bride, a native of this city, was educated at St. Bartholomew's Roman Catholic school in Wiltshire, England, and received her medical degree from the University of Cambridge. The couple will make their home in Milan.

---

NAIVELY, MOM AND CHAZ FIRST TRIED to keep the news from me. They did not realize that the whole world loves this sort of fairy-tale event. It was broadcast on every one of the television channels in the hospital. So I watched it innumerable times in God knows how many languages.

During the next few weeks, my emotions oscillated between in-credulity and paranoia. At times I prayed this was all a nightmare from which I would ultimately wake and, to my enormous relief, find everything the way it was.

At the height of my insanity, I imagined that those thugs had been hired by Silvia's father to kill me and steal her back.

But most of the time I was bewildered. I did not know what to believe about Silvia, about the world, about myself.

The agony was protracted. For, in the next few weeks, there was no newspaper or magazine anywhere that did not have pictures of them on their honeymoon.

"Matthew," Chaz said as gently as he could. "She's gone. And you've got to come to terms with the fact that you may never find out what really happened. You should just be grateful you're alive and go-ing to make a full recovery."

That's no consolation, I thought to myself. That's a punishment.

LATE ONE AFTERNOON THREE DAYS BEFORE I was discharged, I was sitting by the open door to the terrace, trying to read and get some air. The nurse suddenly entered to announce an unexpected visitor: A young woman who had identified herself merely as "Sarah Conrad, a friend of a friend."

She was undeniably pretty, with short, shiny chestnut hair, gentle eyes and a soft voice. Her educated English accent immediately told me who she was. I sensed why she might have come and asked to be left alone with her. She looked at me—a trifle uneasily, I thought—and at last inquired:

"Are you all right?"

"That depends on who's asking," I answered suspiciously. "Did she send you?"

Sarah nodded.

"Were you at the wedding?"

"Yes."

"Why did she do it?"

She shrugged. "I don't know. I'm not sure she knows herself. I guess it was always in the cards." She seemed to weigh every syllable she spoke with extreme care.

"But that was before Paris—before Africa."

At first she didn't answer. She sat on the edge of her chair like a prim schoolgirl, holding her clenched fists tightly together. She could not look me in the eye, but at last produced an envelope. She got up, handed it to me and started to leave.

"No, wait," I shouted. And then apologetically added, "Please." She sat down again nervously as I tore it open:

*My dearest friend,*

*I owe you my life and an explanation. I will be forever grateful that I spent even a few moments with someone as wonderful as you. I only wish the ending could have been otherwise.*

*At it is, I can only say that I did what I thought was right. For both of us.*

*Please forget me. I am sure you will find the happiness you*

*deserve. I will treasure the joy of our encounter for the rest of my
life.*

*Love,*

*Silvia*

Up to this point—I now realized—I had not completely given up
hope. But Silvia's own hand had destroyed the last refuge of my self-
delusion. I addressed Sarah in defeat:

"Tell me honestly, how did they make her marry him?"

"There was no gun at her head," she replied almost in a whisper.
Then reddened, obviously regretting her choice of metaphor.

Unrealistically I hoped that if I interrogated her long enough I
would get the secret out of her.

Sarah sensed this, but despite my persistent questioning, she remained steadfast. Unshakenly loyal to Silvia. At last she stood up.

"It was nice meeting you," she said awkwardly. "I mean, I'm glad
to know you're going to be all right. If there's anything you need . . ."

She didn't finish the thought. Clearly she had been about to devi-
ate from the approved script.

"Can't I give you some kind of answer to take back to her?"

She gestured helplessly.

"So this is it?" I demanded as much to myself as to her. "We meet,
we fall in love and then she just disappears from the planet without so
much as a goodbye?"

"I'm sorry, Matthew," Sarah murmured. "But you're not the only
one in pain."

She began to walk slowly off and I called after her, "What do you
mean by that? What the hell do you mean?"

She stopped and turned around again. I was surprised to see she was now on the brink of tears. "She was right, Matthew. You're everything she said you were."

Then she was gone. And I was alone with Silvia's final words.

WHEN THEY FINALLY DECLARED ME well enough to leave the hospital, Professor Tammuz himself gave me strict orders to take things easy and avoid all stressful situations. In his usual erudite manner, he observed that the ancients were correct. Two millennia had not produced a cure better than Hippocrates' notion that the greatest of all healers was time.

"Matthew is still unsteady on his feet," the doctor lectured my family. "He tires easily and needs to regain his strength—mental as well as physical."

My brother and I took Mom to the airport. She hugged me goodbye and, with obvious misgivings, boarded the plane back to Michigan. We had convinced her that Malcolm needed her. And since Ellen, safely into her second trimester, was staying with her parents, Chaz was the logical person to keep me company.

Two hours later we were on a train streaking across the country.

Where is this place you're taking me?" I demanded irritably. My brother was a saint to put up with this cantankerous behavior, but somehow I couldn't help finding fault with everything. "Switzerland has a surplus of two things: cuckoo clocks and mountains. So why do we have to go all this way just to see another overgrown hill?"

"First of all, the trip itself is beautiful," he began patiently. "Secondly, we're going practically to the roof of the world, where you can see all the way to the Matterhorn. Third, there's absolutely nothing to do there but walk, relax and look at snow."

"It's too early," I grumbled. "There won't be any snow."

"There always is on the glacier," he replied triumphantly. "I'm sure you'll begin to sleep and put some weight back on. Most important, you might even find the person you're looking for."

"Yeah? Who?"

"Yourself, you idiot."

WE GOT OFF THE TRAIN AT SION and walked two blocks to the funicular railroad, which went straight up, and a mere twenty minutes later, deposited us a mile higher in the town of Crans-Montana.

Whether by chance or design, the Hotel du Parc had in the early part of the century been a sanitorium for tuberculosis. An atmosphere of recuperation somehow permeated the halls. It also commanded a reverential view of the Matterhorn.

Despite the claim that thin air at altitude keeps you awake the first few nights, the moment we reached our room I leaned back on the bed and fell asleep fully clothed. The last thing I remember was Chaz pulling off my shoes.

"That's it, big brother, relax. We're at the magic mountain now. You're going to get better. I know you are."

EVEN THE MOST INVETERATE MISANTHROPE would have his pessimism shaken at the sight of a massive snowcapped peak refulgent in the bright summer sun. This was the view from our terrace at breakfast. The bread had come from the baker across the street, the butter from a neighboring cow and the cheese imported from the next village.

Like two schoolboys we "used up" the extra rolls in our *panier* to make our own picnic lunch, which we planned to eat yet another mile higher on the glacier.

When we had stepped off the cable car at three thousand meters, the air was thin and I felt short of breath. Before us stretched a vast concave plain covered with snow.

Ever the conscientious tour guide, Chaz pointed out the more attractive skiers in the minimalist bikinis.

"So what," I said sourly. "You're married and I don't give a damn. Let's eat lunch." Chaz laughed.

"What's the matter?" I demanded.

"Do you realize it's only ten o'clock? Anyway, it's nice to see you're hungry."

AFTER A WEEK OF WANDERING through tranquil forests, past unspoiled lakes above even the smallest towns and villages, I began to regain some strength. My inner bruises seemed to hurt a little less.

I suggested to my brother that we rent skis.

"But Professor Tammuz said to take it easy."

"Come on, the glacier is as flat as a pancake. If there's any place I can ski, it's here."

Though my legs were still a little unsure at first, I found I could stand up and by noon was gliding respectably. It was exhilarating. I could tell Chaz was quietly pleased.

A FEW DAYS LATER we were walking through the main square, looking for a place to have lunch, when I caught sight of a poster outside the church, announcing the forthcoming piano recital by the fabled Vladimir Horowitz. Crans, strategically located between Geneva and Milan, attracts an extremely cosmopolitan crowd.

That afternoon, in the middle of the starkly white-walled sanctuary, stood a platform graced by a magnificent ebony grand piano polished to perfection.

As the time of the concert approached, I began to feel excited. I had not heard live music in so long (in fact most of the music I had "listened" to these past few months had been played in my head as I exercised on my silent keyboard).

At four o'clock the small church was packed. Horowitz walked on stage, bone-thin and stoop-shouldered. He had a birdlike face and appeared nervous.

That is, until he was at the piano. The moment he sat down, he emanated supreme confidence even before playing the first note.

It was an unforgettable experience. I have never heard anyone play so delicately, and at the same time convey so much emotion. For a fleeting instant I almost regretted my career decision long ago.

His varied program demonstrated that he feared no style of composition. His renditions were stunning and his speed—never without feeling—exhilarating. One sensed that part of his artistry was to demonstrate how very fast a human being could play and still remain a musician and not a mere sprinter.

The allegretto movement of Mozart's piano sonata was swift enough. Chopin's scherzo was even faster. But the pièce de résistance was his finale by Moritz Moszkowski, a little-known Prussian composer whose Etude in F—all of a minute and a half—left both audience and soloist breathless.

And his encore was both a surprise and thrill for me. It was Horowitz's own arrangement of John Philip Sousa's "Stars and Stripes Forever" played with such velocity and panache that when he imitated the piccolo obbligato in the grand finale, it sounded as though he had three hands. I was first on my feet, cheering both out of patriotism and sheer worship of the man's genius.

The ambiance of the church had made the audience into a sort of congregation. Unbidden, many of them felt impelled to come up and shake the maestro's hand—an experience, his face betrayed, to which he was not ordinarily accustomed. As I stood there waiting my turn, I glanced at the ivory keys of the magnificent Steinway with the lust of a man who has been on a desert island seeing a voluptuous woman for the first time.

Chaz could not help but notice my fixation and whispered, "Stick around and play after he goes."

Horowitz finally escaped his well-wishers and a few moments later the hall was empty. Now it was just Chaz and myself and the piano.

"Aren't they going to lock it?"

"This is a village," he answered. "Nobody locks anything. Go on, give yourself a treat. I've got to buy some postcards. I'll meet you back at the hotel."

It looked so tempting. I sat on the bench for a long time, not daring to touch the keys. At first I wondered what I should play.

And then I wondered what I *could* play.

Slowly, with mounting horror, I realized the answer: nothing. Absolutely nothing.

It was then I knew that I could perhaps survive the loss of Silvia. But the music was irretrievably gone.

From my hands. From my head. From my heart.

# FOURTEEN

I FELT ALMOST INVISIBLE as I moved through the crowd of merrymaking tourists chatting animatedly about the dinners they were going out to have.

I made up my mind to tell no one about my inner muteness. I would not burden anyone else.

Back at the hotel I did my best to make lively conversation during our meal, well aware that sooner or later Chaz would ask me the painful question. As we were sitting peacefully on the porch later that evening, he inquired:

"How'd it go?"

"What?"

"Your reunion with the keyboard."

I moved my right hand from side to side to indicate "so-so."

He was unperturbed. "Give yourself a chance. It'll all come back."

He didn't know. How could he?

AFTER A FEW DAYS OF QUIET BROODING I came to a decision. I would stop mourning. I would not be a source of pain to my family. If they hadn't been around, I suppose I would have thrown myself off one of the more picturesque cliffs. But now Ellen was going to make me an uncle. And it was time to stop hiding in this fantasy world where the scenery was too beautiful to be real.

Chaz had succeeded in convincing me that Scott Fitzgerald's motto (borrowed from George Herbert) was right: living well is the best revenge.

"In your case," he added, with the new maturity acquired from his ordeal, "I would settle for just plain living for a start."

I tried to smile. That facial response so necessary for normal social intercourse was something I would have to master again.

LATER THAT DAY I BEGAN TO ACT on my decision. My brother stood by in dismay as I threw my clothes into a suitcase.

"You're not serious, are you?" he demanded. "You're not really going back to Africa?"

"Well, I can see you're still not too old to learn something from your big brother, Chaz. It's called honoring your commitments. I signed on for three years and by God I saw how badly they needed me. I'm going back to where I can do some good."

He could tell I was immovable and resigned himself to the task of helping me prepare for my return to the wilderness. We had plenty of spending money, since all medical bills had been covered by Médecine Internationale, who had also continued to pay my salary while I was in the hospital. So I bought presents for everybody, including a bottle of geneva (normal size) for Maurice.

It was only when we were sitting in the departure lounge and we heard the last call for my flight that Chaz grew agitated. Actually he had been so strong during what must have been an emotional crucible for him. We had grown even closer after I had come within a hair's breadth of immortality, a fact that he had succeeded in denying until this moment.

I patted him on the shoulder.

"Don't worry, Chaz, I'll come back in one piece, I promise you."

"You said that last time." He smiled wryly.

"And I did, didn't I? Give Ellen a special kiss from me."

We embraced and I did not turn to look back as I boarded the plane.

NO SOONER WERE WE AIRBORNE than I realized that I had forgotten to bring a present for François. Fortunately I was able to rectify this grave oversight while changing planes in Cairo. For twenty-five dollars I got him a plaster model of the Sphinx. The only trouble was he couldn't smoke or drink it, but at least it showed thought.

And as he had promised on the phone when he jubilantly received the news that I had booked my flight back, he himself was waiting for me right on the tarmac in Asmara.

As I descended the first few steps, I was barely able to breathe. This was not, as it once had been, a journey to the unknown. It was a return to the all too familiar.

François threw his arms around me.

Though I protested my health and strength, he insisted upon carrying my bags to the car. But his most generous gesture was abstaining from smoking out of respect for the current Swiss purity of my lungs.

During the journey he filled me in on almost every event: the changes of personnel and even the most minor incidents that had occurred in my absence. It was something of a bravura performance that he never once mentioned Silvia's name.

And as the rest of the evening proved, her vanishing act was complete. For she had been expunged from everyone else's vocabulary as well.

"We've missed you," François stated in a tone surprisingly devoid of his usual sardonic humor. "It was only in your absence that I realized how valuable you were.

"Anyway," he said, slapping my thigh, "with you we're back at full strength again. I managed to get this Australian fellow I had short-listed."

"How is he?" I asked.

"As a doctor, first-rate. As a human being, zero. Apparently the rumor that humility doesn't flourish very well Down Under is true. He's not as irresistible as he thinks he is, but by the time he arrived Denise was such an emotional pushover she convinced herself that he was the answer to all her prayers. Otherwise his ego would have died of malnourishment. Actually, having someone in common to hate has been very good for morale."

As usual, François's social observations were right on target.

Everyone was waiting up for my return, and there were bottles of local St. George's beer and some generous soul had even offered the last quarter bottle of duty-free whisky.

One by one they all came up and hugged me. All except a big muscular-looking guy who merely offered his simian hand and introduced himself in a broad Australian accent.

"Doug Maitland, Junior," he announced. (As if I might have

known Doug Maitland, Senior.) "Too bad I wasn't there when you got winged, mate," he stated modestly. "I could have sorted you out right on the spot."

"Oh," I inquired. "Are you a brain surgeon?"

"No, orthopedics. But I know my way around the skull, and from what I hear you didn't get it too badly. Anyway, mate, it's good to have you on board."

Wait a minute, I thought to myself. That's my line, or did he now think he had been there first too? François must have had to dig very deep from his list of alternates to come up with this character.

It was good to see everyone. Even taciturn Marta gave me a big kiss, as did Aida, who was especially touched by the perfume I had brought her.

Yet I had managed to travel several thousands of miles from Zurich, avoiding any thoughts about what really awaited me at the end.

François had not changed the sleeping arrangements while I was gone. I was given a flashlight and Gilles helped me carry my stuff to hut number eleven. He left me at the door and I entered alone. It was musty inside, but then it might always have been. I had never paid attention to such climatic nuances in my previous stay there.

I flashed my light over to the bed. It was neatly made with a light sheet and blanket folded at the foot. Scarcely three months ago we were here together making love, and now I was alone and it was as if she had never existed. I was drawn to the cupboards that had been hastily constructed for us. I opened the drawers on the right. My clothes were exactly where I had left them. I opened the other side. Hers were still there too. Only the heartbeat, the voice, the person was missing.

How the hell would I sleep there tonight?

The answer was—with difficulty.

IN MY ABSENCE some new interpersonal dynamics had developed within the group. It seemed our Australian colleague had joined us with a sense of entitlement even larger than his boots. Almost immediately he had begun to lobby for bungalow eleven for himself and Denise. ("What the hell," he argued. "The place is sitting empty. Neither of those guys is coming back.")

To which François had responded, "When I'm convinced of that, I'll consider reassigning it."

When Doug Maitland, Junior, first arrived, he had been billeted with poor Gilles. It was, to say the least, a clash of cultures. At the height of their ardor, he and Denise seemed to pick the most inconvenient times to ask Gilles to absent himself. Or, as Doug put it, "Go looking for that prize dodo of yours."

I immediately offered to move back into my old bunk, but François was adamant.

"That would teach the Australian nothing. But if you do want to help Gilles, it would be generous if you would allow him to share hut eleven with you."

"Sure," I replied. "I would hate to give that antipodean any satisfaction."

As it turned out, both parties claimed victory. Which, as François confided to me, is one of the secrets of good leadership.

NATURALLY DRESSER SPACE had to be cleared to make room for Gilles. That licensed François to have Silvia's belongings given away to where they would do most good.

It didn't take me long to get resynchronized with the routine. The patients had changed, their ailments hadn't. There was still so much needless suffering.

We continued to lose sick people who, under ordinary circumstances, we would have treated on the spot and sent home to live long lives.

Before we sat down to dinner one evening, François cornered me and remarked, "By the way, Matt, tomorrow's Tuesday."

"I'm glad to hear that—especially since today's Monday. I'd be worried if it were otherwise."

"Come on, Matthew, you know what Maurice and I do every Tuesday afternoon."

"Yeah, that's right." It suddenly came back to me. "It's cataract day, isn't it?"

"Yes, and I'd like you to scrub up with us."

"Since when do you need help with a procedure you've done maybe a thousand times?"

"Since this." He held his hands in front of me, and I clearly saw the swelling in the knuckles that was either recent or that I had failed to notice before. It looked ominous.

"What seems to be the problem?" I asked, offering him the courtesy of being able to withhold whatever detail he wanted.

"Go ahead, Matthew. Make the diagnosis. It looks like rheumatoid arthritis, and it is."

"Oh, I'm sorry."

"That's okay. I've had time to get used to this. Fortunately, I enjoy teaching, and frankly I'm looking forward to the bright lights of Paris. Meanwhile, there's a ready solution to the problem out here."

"And that is?"

He looked me in the eye and smiled, "You, *mon cher*. As of tomorrow you begin training to succeed me as cataract surgeon."

"Doug won't like that," I remarked.

"Well, I don't like Doug, so we're even. It's a straightforward operation and our organization has always trained non-surgeons to specialize in just this one ophthalmic procedure. Don't worry, you won't be asked to transplant corneas or anything."

I didn't know how to react. Among other things, I knew this had to be very difficult for someone like François.

"Matthew, why do you look so miserable?" he chided.

"Well, I know this may come as a shock but I actually like you."

"Thanks, but for God's sake don't tell anybody. I don't want to lose my image."

"Shit, how will we manage without you?" I said.

"Very well, I think. They'll be getting a first-rate leader in you."

I returned to the hut that night with completely different thoughts in my head. The day before I had been feeling sorry for myself. Tonight I had something more meaningful to think about:

Feeling sorry for François.

**Cataracts are probably the greatest cause of blindness in the world and the biggest workload. . . . The high prevalence in the underdeveloped world is probably related to high sunlight levels. . . .**

I had been unable to sleep and wandered over to the empty dining room, reheated a mug of last night's brackish coffee and began to read up on my impending surgical specialty.

In places like Eritrea, the incidence of this disease is at least *twenty* times as great as in Europe and America. That is why no team worth its salt goes out into the wilds without a capable (if not Board Certified) eye surgeon.

The next day François was his usual acerbic self, without a trace of self-pity. I'm sure he was aware that I was observing him with new eyes, studying him not merely as a doctor but as a leader. It was only in trying to imagine what it would be like that I realized how incredibly difficult and complex his job really was.

As far as the surgery was concerned, he had not misrepresented. The whole procedure took barely thirty minutes. It was performed under local anesthetic. The incisions were straightforward if delicate. Still, as I assisted him, I began to realize why François had decided to retire himself and I respected him even more for it.

The following Tuesday, with my own hands I restored the sight of five blind people. It was the most thrilling experience of my life. An old man saw his grandchildren for the first time. A woman saw her grown son whom she had last seen as a little boy. And to think François had this experience every single week he was in the field. I could not repress the thought of how sad he must feel at not being able to do it anymore.

The moment he officially turned over the operation to my absolute control, the rumors began to fly. And socially I was in limbo: no longer "one of the peons," but not yet the commander.

The only person who seemed at ease with me was Gilles, who was happy as a lark (so to speak) being my roommate again.

With my eminence imminent, I was now granted a kerosene lamp to allow me to work at night, and which aroused no small amount of envy. (I had no doubt that Doug would be demanding his in the morning.) Of course, the illumination also enabled Gilles to keep up his ornithological reading.

One night as I was going over some records and Gilles was deep in avian research, I looked at his face in the light of the flickering lamp and he seemed somehow different. Gradually the astonishing thought occurred to me that he—unlike all the others in this leaky lifeboat in the middle of the desert—was happier.

"Tell me, is it just having that stupid Aussie off your back?"

"What, Matthew?"

"Did anything happen while I was gone?"

"Well," he hemmed and hawed, "I did take a short holiday. I flew to Kenya."

"Oh, do you have friends there?"

"As a matter of fact, yes. Some of the people who had worked with my mother and father."

"What did they do?"

"My parents were medical missionaries. They died years ago when I was a child. But even before that I lived mostly with an aunt and uncle in France and saw them only when they had home leave. I couldn't understand why they had left me behind. Yet when I finally visited their friends they told me how hard my mother found it to leave me. All those years I had never even imagined that she missed me."

He set his book down and took off his glasses.

"They were killed during the Mau Mau uprisings in the 1950s and I've been bitter ever since. That was until I came here. Now I'm doing what they did, and I see why they sacrificed their lives.

"I visited the school named after them and put some flowers on their graves." He paused for a moment, took a deep breath and said quietly, "Actually, I think when I'm finished here, I'll go to Kenya and continue their work."

I was touched that he had taken me into his confidence. He was now emboldened to pose a question of his own.

"Matthew, could I ask you something? I've been thinking about it a lot."

"What's that?"

"It's about your little piano."

It was bound to come up sooner or later.

"What about it?"

"I never see you play it anymore. Have you given it up for some reason—if I'm not intruding?" he diffidently added.

"No, that's okay," I lied. "I just don't have the time."

I could see I was not convincing him.

"People say you were very good. Very good indeed."

"I guess I was—once."

He sensed that I was unwilling to open the door to my psyche any wider. Yet as he turned over in bed, he could not suppress an involuntary, "That's too bad."

"What is?" I asked, now slightly uncomfortable.

He turned around and looked at me, myopic without his glasses.

"I've been in a room while a great pianist was playing and never heard a note."

EVER SINCE FRANÇOIS HAD TOLD ME months earlier that I would be running the whole show, I had occasional spasms of doubt as to whether I was up to it without him there as a living encyclopedia. Then gradually I found myself almost looking forward to his departure so that I could institute some of my new ideas, especially the public health program I had long been pondering.

During the week before officially taking over, I made a point of having a heart-to-heart conversation with every one of the doctors. I assured them that nothing would change in their jobs unless they wanted it to. (As usual Maitland was the exception. He demanded to do the cataracts and I refused him.) It was gratifying to learn that the team was pleased that I had been selected. Each in his own way promised to help me get through the early difficult days. They were a terrific bunch, their dedication now enhanced by experience. François had chosen well.

On the day he flew home, our boss wanted no hoopla and insisted I keep the clinics open as usual. Only myself and a driver were excused to take him to the airport. The night before, we had ignored doctor's orders and drunk a hell of a lot of rotgut. He could interpret the hangovers we all nursed the next morning as expressions of sadness at his leaving.

THE NEXT EIGHTEEN MONTHS were a time of building. In a way it turned out to be an advantage to have François as our man in Paris. He was closer to the purse strings, and his adept diplomacy managed to get us grants to complete the long-overdue air-conditioning of the consulting rooms.

He performed miracles with the financing of my grandiosely named Public Health Campaign. I was determined to leave something permanent, a benchmark however modest, for the greater health of these long-suffering people. I resolved that in the time left to me I would inoculate every child I could reach against smallpox and polio.

According to my records, by the time I left we had immunized nearly forty thousand children. We also trained twenty-four practical nurses and two mobile clinics to teach basic hygiene.

Gradually we had grown more and more like a family of which—despite my inner unpreparedness—I had to act as patriarch. That year we celebrated Christmas on the orthodox date of January 7 as guests of Aida's village. We had bowls and bowls of *zigini* with all the trimmings.

INTERESTINGLY ENOUGH, in all this time, we had only one defection in the ranks. Doug Maitland, the mighty Australian Tarzan, couldn't take it. No sooner was the ink dry on his CV than strangely the climate began to affect an old rugby injury of his. It soon became, like the man himself, intolerable. Though it would wreak havoc with our work schedules, I let him go with a mere fifteen days' notice.

With characteristic subtlety, he reminded me of the important contribution he had made.

"Listen, mate, I've done my time in this shithole, and I'm counting on you for a bloody good letter."

I hoped he could count to infinity.

Meanwhile, his rapid retreat meant I had some urgent pastoral work to do with Denise. I tried to comfort her by emphasizing that she was worthy of someone better than that bombastic creep.

"It's not over," she protested bravely. "I'll be visiting him in Melbourne."

"Sure you will," I said and tried to sound convincing.

GILLES WAS READY TO DIE HAPPY. He had already told the first two people at breakfast his great news, and the moment he caught sight of me began to wave frantically. Somehow that look of utter triumph on his face could only have meant one thing.

"I saw him, the Northern Bald Ibis. I saw him this morning! Can you imagine how I feel, Matthew?"

"No," I answered honestly. "But it couldn't have happened to a nicer guy. Congratulations."

ERITREA IS A COUNTRY where nothing seems to end. The drought had begun in 1968—more than ten years earlier—and seemed as if it would go on forever. Likewise, the civil war also raged on unabated. The EPLF recovered from the Russian assault in 1978, but there was no sign of either side losing the will to fight or that the conflict would be resolved in the foreseeable future. The famine remained an unaltering fact of life.

This endlessness took its inevitable toll on my staff to whom the morning lines never seemed one patient shorter. And to the trauma team, who were still removing bullets from wounded fighters every day and night.

By the next Christmas, I could see that everyone was dreaming of home. Even I was growing weary of trying to boost their morale while maintaining my own.

As their contracts neared expiration, no one signed up for an extension (if you discount Gilles, who was going to continue his work in Kenya, anyway).

FROM THE TIME WE HAD SPENT TOGETHER in Switzerland, my brother had learned how to win an argument against me without seeming to be arguing. He recognized that my psychic pendulum was currently swinging toward altruism and never once invoked our family—not even my little niece, Jessica—as a possible reason to lure me home.

Instead he pointed out the subtle connection between the new genetic sciences and the medical project I had been running on the ground.

"Just imagine," he wrote. "Someday we won't have to worry about curing diseases like diabetes because they won't exist. Instead of manufacturing insulin for those who lack it, the new techniques now replace the genes in the body that should be doing it naturally. Don't you want a piece of this action?"

I was hooked again.

And I guess Chaz knew it when I asked him to send more stuff.

During the last six months of my contract, I applied to various universities to pursue a doctorate in molecular biology. My rather special field experience obviously made a positive impression on the schools I applied to because they all accepted me.

I decided to go to Harvard purely so I wouldn't have to spend the rest of my medical career explaining to people why I hadn't. There I had the privilege of studying with Max Rudolph and his successor, Adam Coopersmith.

THE NIGHT BEFORE I LEFT, we had the traditional drunken revel with mocking speeches and lugubrious farewells. I was already feeling nostalgic but tried not to show it.

With such an early flight I would really have no time next morning to say a proper farewell to the most important there: the patients. So after closing my luggage and tying up my books, I strolled over and visited the various campfires of those waiting to be seen the next morning.

By now, speaking Tigrinya practically as well as I spoke English, I could trade quips with them. I recognized a pregnant woman I treated whose first child had died from dysentery.

I wished her all sorts of better luck with her new one. She thanked me for my kindness. I kissed her goodbye and walked back to the hut.

Gilles was waiting anxiously for my return.

"Hey, look, Matthew, you almost forgot this," he said, holding up my silent keyboard.

"That's okay," I said. "I don't need it anymore."

"But what should we do with it? It would be a shame just to throw it out."

I agreed and suggested to him that he give it as a gift from me to the pregnant lady sitting at the nearby fire. I could tell he was baffled about what *she* would do with it. But then he looked on the bright side and said:

"Perhaps it will inspire her child to become a virtuoso."

"You never know." I smiled and walked inside.

I STILL MISS THE PEOPLE, the patients, even the tortured countryside. And when I said goodbye to my Eritrean friends, I felt very sad and ashamed at leaving them to go back to a place where I could put my feet up, open a beer and watch *Wide World of Sports*.

A little more than two months before my own leave-taking, we broke ground for a twenty-four-bed hospital with a well-equipped O.R. It may not seem like much in the great scheme of things, I know. But, goddammit, it was a start.

And if there is one thing that I brought back from my total experience in Eritrea, it was that *I made a difference.*

PART THREE

# NEW YORK
# 1981

# FIFTEEN

THERE IS A POPULAR LEGEND about a graduate student who entered the genetic engineering lab at Harvard twenty years ago and has never emerged. Some say he is still there, eyes welded to an electron microscope, desperately seeking a particularly fugitive gene. There is a certain truth to this, for once a researcher begins such a quest part of him remains forever bonded to that phantasmagoric world where there is no day, no night, no change of season or passage of time.

When I started at Harvard, the field was virtually in its infancy. It had been less than twenty years since Crick and Watson discovered the structure of DNA, providing a key that would in time unlock every single secret of the body's seventy-five trillion cells.

Yet there were already visionaries who believed

that all diseases would ultimately be cured by the infusion of a corrected version of whatever gene had been found defective.

I was one of those dedicated zealots. I was convinced it could be done, should be done and if none of us got any sleep for the rest of our lives—*would* be done.

I spent the first four years after my return from Africa rooted in front of my DNA synthesizer, running trial after trial, searching for the precise molecular combination that could be used to reverse a tumor.

My obsessive search for a single gene reminded me of Gilles, freezing at five o'clock every morning, scanning the horizon for a glimpse of an elusive bird. And my compulsion to vanquish disease kept me up all night.

Can man survive on pizza alone? For years philosophers have debated the question. But as a graduate student I tested it empirically. I knew that in Eritrea man could live on *injara* and little else. How infinitely richer was a diet of a similar flat bread enhanced by melted cheese and sliced tomato?

Some may wonder at the relevance of this to scientific research. The answer is, when you're in hot pursuit of a specific strand of DNA, you don't waste time on dinner or whatever meal the hour warrants. Pizza is the be-all and end-all.

THE PROJECT FOR MY DISSERTATION WAS, not unsurprisingly, in the realm of neurobiology. When you have been shot in the head it is no exaggeration to say that your brain is often on your mind. Thus I took to searching the cerebral hemispheres, exploring neural pathways, leaping across synapses to see what I could find in this still little-known domain. This inner Eden was also a place where monsters sometimes came to sow their tumors of destruction. I became increasingly committed to destroying them.

AFTER FINISHING MY RESEARCH in molecular biology in 1984, I stayed at Harvard as a postdoctoral fellow. I guess inertia had a lot to do with it. Labs look pretty much the same everywhere, and Boston seemed as good a place as any to eat pizza.

Besides, on the rare occasions we did eat out, I always conned my buddies into going to the North End, the old Italian section of town, where you barely saw a sign or heard a word in English.

Every time I went there I imagined I saw Silvia. Sometimes I thought I heard her voice or glimpsed her walking just ahead of me. I hurried to catch up only to realize that my mind was playing tricks again.

Even now at night I dreamed that she reappeared, only to wake and find myself alone. I guess it wasn't simply the pursuit of science that kept me locked up in the lab.

AS I BEGAN TO PUBLISH MY FINDINGS, I received various inquiries from institutions sounding out my willingness to move. One particularly attractive offer came from Cornell Medical School in uptown Manhattan.

By this time Chaz was near despair, certain I was turning into a "frumpy old bachelor." He was anxious for me to move anywhere hoping that, en route from one microscope to another, I might meet a nice stewardess and live happily ever after. Ellen, who was just as concerned about my sentimental lethargy, expressed it with a little more subtlety:

"In Boston the right woman is there if you can find her. In New York, even if you're trying to avoid her, she'll find *you*."

Chaz touted New York's infinite cultural opportunities—theater, concerts, operas and the like. Not to mention that the eminence surrounding the job would be a lodestone to the best and brightest women.

In any case, I decided to go. It was time for a change. I finally had overcome the guilt of living in a place with more than one room in it. I was especially lucky to find this really nice apartment on East End Avenue with a view of the river that inspired me to begin jogging (my waistline appeared to be advancing even faster than my career).

The place was ideally situated, the price surprisingly reasonable. And yet it had been on the market for nearly six months. Mrs. Osterreicher, the elderly lady selling it, was being extraordinarily fastidious about whom she would allow to live in the flat she had shared for so many years with her psychoanalyst husband.

For some reason (desperation?) she smiled at me the minute I walked into the room and, apparently uncharacteristically, volunteered to show me around herself.

And yet she was unable to allow herself to enter her husband's study, remaining uneasily at the doorway as I admired the floor-to-ceiling wooden shelves, crammed with professional and belletristic literature in various European languages.

"If you are at all interested in any of the books, Doctor . . ." she began timidly, but could not finish the sentence.

"Aren't you taking them?" I asked, responding with immediate empathy to the sadness in her voice.

"I'm going to Florida to live with my daughter. But they have more than enough books already—"

She stopped herself when she noticed my gaze had discovered the piano.

It was one of those mahogany "parlor grands" they used to make before the war, magnificently finished, its ivory keys almost pristine. And instinctively I knew it was still in perfect tune.

"Do you play?" I heard her inquire.

"I used to." The tone of a Sunday golfer.

And now she was at my elbow, smiling warmly and gesturing toward the instrument.

"Would you honor me, Doctor?" There was such longing in her tone.

I was paralyzed for an instant, caught between the overwhelming desire to play—for myself as much as for her—and the terrifying certainty that I still no longer could.

I looked down at the keyboard. And suddenly I was atop those dizzying cliffs in Mexico, the ones that tempt the daredevils to risk their lives. I seemed to be up so high that the mere sight of the black and white keys made me vertiginous. My heart began to race. I backed slowly away from the edge.

"I'm sorry," I mumbled. "I'm a bit out of practice."

Despite my enormous desire to escape, I forced myself to be polite and remain as long as possible. She continued to talk, but somehow I did not hear a word she was saying. At the first decent opportunity, I fled.

WHEN I RETURNED TO THE HOSPITAL there was a message already waiting for me. It was from the agent: "Mrs. Osterreicher would like to include the piano in whatever price you offer for her apartment. Grab it before they put her in the loony bin."

———

THERE IS NO WORD THAT precisely denotes the opposite of a nightmare. "Daydream" does not quite fit because I enjoyed this almost sensual fantasy while I was sleeping that same night.

I was seated at Dr. Osterreicher's piano. The room was dark and hushed. The hour was late and I was completely alone. Then I began to play. It was easy, as effortless as breathing. From the artless, simple Prelude in C Major, I moved naturally through the rest of the *Well-Tempered Clavier,* the partitas, sonatas, flawlessly performing the *Art of the Fugue.* And then I began again with the Prelude in C Major, in an endlessly repeating journey through the complete keyboard works of the great master.

Both my body and soul were consumed with love. I was not only playing music again, I was united with it. It was the happiest moment of my life.

Then I awoke. If the joy of the dream had been exquisite, the pain of the reality was even more so. I now knew for certain that I would never be able to play that beautiful piano.

The next morning I called Mrs. Osterreicher to thank her for agreeing to sell her apartment to me and especially for her generous offer of the piano, which I unfortunately could not accept. She replied politely that she understood, but sounded heartbroken.

AND SO I MOVED DOWN FROM BOSTON in June when the early evenings were still cool enough to tempt the novice jogger.

I even found a cleaning lady to pick up the various socks and jocks from the floor, and made some semblance of tidiness. Often I would come home to find that she had left me some nutritious dinner to heat up in the microwave, along with an admonitory note like:

*Dear Doctor, health begins at home. Yours, Mary Beth.*

My contract provided two personal laboratory assistants who definitely speeded up the output of my work. I also spent three afternoons a week as a pediatric neurologist. Though in the main I was dealing with cases for whom unfortunately we could offer only a diagnosis and nothing more, I enjoyed the personal interaction with my young patients. This also served to remind me why I was doing all my research.

By the late 1980s, genetic engineering was finally producing some concrete results. In my own case I had developed a technique for activating specific killer T-cells which destroyed certain tumor growths in mice.

Not that it was all work and no play. I mean, at least once a year I found myself in exotic places like Acapulco, Honolulu and Tokyo (my colleagues really know how to pick sites for their conventions). And I *had* to go because I was now Chairman.

These occasions provided what passed for a social life in those years: the occasional quickie romance. I guess some of these women were real possibilities. But I didn't take things further because, despite whatever gifts of mind and personality they might have had, they weren't Silvia.

WE WERE ALL IN SUCH A HURRY THEN. And I think French Anderson, one of the pioneers in our field, best expressed the urgency we all felt: "Ask the cancer patient who has only a few months to live. Ask the AIDS patient whose body is shriveling. . . . The 'rush' arises from our human compassion for our fellow man who needs help now."

But if our branch of medicine was ever to take wing, the bureaucrats in Washington had to find the courage to allow us to try out our therapies on human beings.

All sorts of moral as well as medical issues were involved. The notion of tampering with God's work was one doctrinal objection. There was also the legitimate fear that, since the body contained at least one hundred thousand genes, we might activate the wrong one by error and create some neoplasmic nightmare.

And yet, until we could find someone from the FDA willing to take a leap of faith, our struggle would remain a drama with no final act. The deliberating panels always managed to sidestep the issue till it became academic, i.e., the patient had died. Someone had to force them to let us intervene while there was still a breath of time. It fell to my lot to do just that.

I MET JOSH LIPTON, a charming, tousled-haired eleven-year-old, when he was on his deathbed. He had been transferred from Houston where the medulloblastoma growing remorselessly in his brain had already been unsuccessfully attacked with chemotherapy, radiology and surgery. He now had at most a few more weeks to live.

Though every arrow in the quiver of medical science had been exhausted on his behalf, both Josh and his parents were fighters. And, as he clung tenaciously to life, they continued to look for other possible methods, even exploring alternatives among the unorthodox therapies offered by "the clinics for the desperate" just across the Mexican border.

I decided to appeal to Washington to treat Josh on a compassionate dispensation. I got two world experts to submit affidavits stating that this little boy was beyond all known medical help. And since it would cause no further pain or damage, they urged the governmental honchos to let us try my procedure, which—at least in laboratory experiments—had succeeded in reducing tumor growth.

As the government sanctimoniously debated and discussed, Josh's life was quickly ebbing away. I examined him late one afternoon and realized that the next document to this endless paper chase would be a death certificate.

Though I did not know the man personally, I called the Chairman of the committee, Dr. Stephen Grabiner, and laid it on the line:

"Do you want me to read the FDA approval at his funeral, dammit? Get serious, will you, Doctor. Take a chance. It's my neck, not yours." (Actually, it was Josh's neck, but in the heat of these battles patients sometimes find themselves pushed to the periphery.)

Something seemed to be happening at the other end of the wire. A heart had informed a mind, which had awakened a will.

"Point taken, Dr. Hiller. I'll see if I can convene the committee over the weekend."

IT IS CURIOUS THE TRIVIAL DETAILS you remember about momentous events. It was nearly three A.M. on Thursday, March 14, 1991. We were sitting in the lab about to sample a new culinary delicacy, a smoked salmon pizza that I had ordered specially from Le Mistral, when the phone rang for me. I dared to think that at this hour of the night it could not be anything insignificant.

"Hey, Matthew, it's Steve Grabiner. I'm sorry to call you so late, but I knew you wouldn't want me to wait until morning. I won't bore you with the details, but the bottom line is that we're granting you permission to do it *once.* No rematches or encores promised. I'll fax you confirmation in the morning."

I was speechless. "Dr. Grabiner—Steve—what can I say?"

"Well," he replied with a lighthearted weariness, "you can tell me that you're absolutely sure there's no way this could turn into a horror show."

"Well, I can't, you know that."

"That's why I'm going to have a very large scotch and go to sleep. Good night, old buddy."

AS I SCRIBBLED A LIST of staff members to wake up, the qualms began. I had taken on the responsibility of a human being's life on a voyage to the unknown. And though Josh's parents had sworn to me that they held out no false expectations, I could not bear the thought of what my failure would do to them.

Time was so precious that I phoned the on-duty nurse in Josh's ward to have his parents summoned immediately to sign the Informed Consent. She replied that Mr. and Mrs. Lipton were already in their son's room.

Obsessively aware of every particle of sand slipping through the hourglass, I sprinted across the courtyard into the elevator whose numbers were moving with excruciating slowness tonight.

When I reached Josh's floor I dashed toward his room. Barbara and Greg Lipton were now waiting outside in the corridor. There was an air of festivity that seemed unsettlingly premature.

"Oh, Dr. Hiller, this is such wonderful news," Barbara said excitedly.

"Thanks, Doctor," the father acknowledged with more sobriety. "You got us another chance."

I knew the toughest part of my job would be to preserve confidence while not totally extinguishing doubt. A fine line, but I had to tread it. They, no less than I, had to be prepared for failure.

The boy was already awake, and we exchanged a few friendly words while Resa, my senior lab assistant, prepared the apparatus.

I asked my young patient if he knew what this was all about.

"My dad says it's another at-bat, a new drug or something."

"Not exactly a drug," I explained. "It's just a way I've worked out to rearrange the cells in your blood so they'll go back inside you and gobble up that tumor once and for all."

He nodded sleepily as I took the syringe from the tray. I reached for the boy's emaciated arm and tried to find a vein that had not been ravaged. I went in as gently as I could and then drew blood.

Resa then hurried back to the lab, where two other assistants were waiting to begin the slow, tricky, and as yet unproven, process of manipulating his T-cells to induce them to attack the tumor.

BY SIX A.M. THE APPARATUS in my lab was humming and the stimulation was under way. This would all take time, the one thing in short supply. With nothing to do, I merely walked up and down the lab. Resa was the only one who had the guts to upbraid me.

"For God's sake, Matt, can't you find somewhere else to pace? You're getting on everybody's nerves."

Just then the phone rang. It was Warren Oliver, the hospital Press Officer.

"Hey, Hiller, what's happening?"

I was hardly in the mood to make my anxieties public, so I tried to dodge him. But he persevered.

"What's this I hear about you getting the go-ahead from the boys in D.C.? That's news, man. That's great news."

"Only if it works."

"It will, won't it? Besides, even if it doesn't, we can get some mileage just out of you being the first to be granted the permission."

I tried to keep my temper and reminded myself that he was in the business of getting column inches into newspapers, which was fast becoming a medical specialty.

"I'm sorry, Warren, I've really got my hands full right now."

"Well, just don't forget I'm here, Matthew. And we're a team. You're the inside man and I'm the outside man."

I hung up on his pep talk and vowed not to do unto my lab staff what Warren was doing unto me..

I let it be known that I was going out of the hospital for breakfast and would not be back for several hours. They did not disguise their gratitude.

THREE DAYS LATER, we completed the retroviral gene transfer and the new cells were ready to be introduced into the sick boy's bloodstream. Though officially no one knew what was about to happen, there was a palpable tension even in the corridor outside his room.

The parents stood on either side of Josh's pillow, holding their son's hands, as I sat on the bed and began to infuse the magic potion—as I referred to it for the boy's sake—into his vein. I tried to look confident.

"How do the cells know exactly where to go, Doctor?" Barbara asked me afterward. "Isn't there a chance that they might get lost in a different part of the body?"

That was the nightmare version. "Well," I answered evasively, "each one has a specific DNA address. I'm hoping that my virus has the right zip code."

THE PATIENT HAD NO IMMEDIATE REACTION, positive or negative.

We entered the phase of watchful waiting.

In the days that followed, I almost never left the hospital except to jog and collect my mail. I came to see Josh about half a dozen times a day, and went through the motions of checking vital signs, examining his eyes, etc.

At one point his father cornered me and tried to clutch for straws of information. "Where are we, Doctor?"

"It's much too early to tell anything, Greg."

"Then why do you keep examining him?" he asked.

How could I answer truthfully that I just wanted to check that his son was still alive?

At the end of the fifth day, we took Josh to radiology for his first postinfusion scan. We all crowded around Al Redding, the radiologist, as he strained to dictate his findings into a microcassette recorder.

"Tumor measures at one-point-five by two by two, which, compared with previous reading on the fourteenth, indicates no net growth."

Murmurs among the onlookers.

"Did I hear you right, Al?" I demanded just to be absolutely sure I had not imagined it. "Are you suggesting that the tumor isn't any larger?"

"I believe that's what I've just reported, Matthew," Redding answered deadpan, as he moved aside so I could take a closer look.

At this moment, I indulged in a wild burst of hope. Yet I did not have the courage to share it with anyone, not even his parents, whose reaction was the polar opposite of our cautious radiologist.

Barbara began to sob quietly. "You've done it, Doctor. It's not growing anymore."

"We can't say that for certain yet," I warned. "Besides, as long as there's a trace of tumor, there's always the risk of hemorrhage. We're not out of the woods yet. This could just be a temporary remission. Meanwhile, I'm going to infuse some more of the new cells we've made."

But now *I* was optimistic. Cautiously optimistic.

THE SCAN FOUR DAYS LATER showed not merely stasis but a twenty-percent reduction in the size of the tumor. It was getting harder to hide my elation, especially when, at the end of the second week, Josh was able to sit up in bed and dangle his feet over the side.

"Do you play tennis, kiddo?" I asked him the morning I gave him his third infusion.

"A little," he answered.

"Well, you and I should make a date to play."

"When?" the boy returned, clearly aware of what he was really asking.

"Well, just as soon as you can walk comfortably."

"Okay, Doc." He smiled. And this time I could distinguish optimism in his eyes.

The miracle occurred three nights later. I was finishing my rounds and thought I would drop by and visit Josh. I turned a corner and could not believe what I saw. At the far end of the corridor my patient was walking with his parents. *Without holding on to either one.*

It was an unbelievable sight and I was overwhelmed. I rushed over to him.

"How do you feel?" I asked breathlessly.

"Okay, Doctor. Cool."

"He's more than okay, he's terrific," laughed Greg. It was the most overt display of sentiment I had ever seen from him.

We didn't stand on ceremony and request an appointment. I simply told a nurse to inform radiology that we would be bringing the kid up for a scan immediately. And they didn't keep us waiting.

The results were sensational. The tumor had shrunk to half its former size and was no longer pressing against the brain.

The phlegmatic Al Redding finally defrosted his emotions and shook my hand vigorously. "*Mazel tov,* Matt. You've done it."

"No, Al. It's Josh who deserves the credit."

BACK IN MY OFFICE, I called the various people in my life: my mother and Malcolm, Chaz and Ellen were all thrilled beyond words. The instant I set the phone down, it suddenly rang again loudly.

"Now what's the story, Matthew?" Warren Oliver asked impatiently. "These reporters are conduits to our contributors. In case you've forgotten, our research programs cost money. And I especially owe a favor to the gal from the *New York Times.* Come on," he urged. "Play the game. Tell me, have you got anything significant to report?"

"Not yet," I answered, thinking in my own mind that one success is not sufficient scientific proof. "Anything I tell you might inspire false hopes."

"Did you just say 'inspire'? You mean you're holding back something positive on me? For God's sake, Matthew, *give.*"

I was defeated, and against my better judgment, agreed to go down to Oliver's office to be interviewed for fifteen minutes and give a sound bite or two.

The journalists were all professionals, mostly M.D.s themselves. While they were impressed by what I told them, I felt reassured that the details would not be sensationalized.

This publicity meant nothing to me.

With one bizarre exception.

I suddenly wondered if the story would be picked up by Italian papers.

# SIXTEEN

IT WAS CLEAR that I had no escape. The press seemed to have gotten hold of every possible number at which I could be reached. My only course of action would be to turn off my pager, duck into a movie and hide.

Or a concert. As I leafed through the Sunday *New York Times,* I studied the multitude of musical treats on offer. Yet I knew immediately which one I would attend.

That very afternoon at Carnegie Hall, Roger Josephson, my old pal Evie's cellist husband, was playing Mozart, Chopin and Franck. She would doubtless be in the audience, and I could not only catch up on her news but share my own.

The place was almost sold out, but I managed to get a single at the far end of the first row. Josephson had put on some weight since the wedding and his hair was streaked with gray. His more distinguished aspect matched the greater maturity of his musical technique. He seemed to be approaching real virtuosity.

As an erstwhile accompanist, I could not help but notice the skill of his pianist, an attractive Mexican woman named Carmen de la Rochas. The two had obviously played together a lot, as their sophisticated phraseology and imaginative rubato demonstrated.

I looked for Evie during the intermission, but it was crowded and besides she might be one of those wives who are too nervous to sit out front, and take refuge in their husbands' dressing rooms.

Roger and his partner played an exciting last movement to the Chopin, amply earning the rapturous applause they received.

I don't usually have the guts to do this sort of thing, but in my euphoria I walked to the stage door, identified myself as a friend of the Josephson family and had no trouble getting myself admitted.

Naturally the cellist's dressing room was packed with toadies and well-wishers, managers, publicists and the like. I was a bit hesitant to dive into that high-powered mob and instead stood on tiptoes to see if I could spot Evie from afar. At this moment the Mexican pianist approached me and asked with a very alluring smile, "May I help you?"

"Thanks," I replied. "I'm an old friend of Mrs. Josephson and I wonder—"

"*I'm* Mrs. Josephson," she reacted with a spark of Latin possessiveness. It took me about a second to catch on.

"But—what happened to Evie?" I responded somewhat gauchely.

"*I* did," she grinned, her dark eyes flashing. "They've been divorced for several years now. Don't you read the papers?"

"Uh, actually, I've been out of the country for a while," I explained with an apologetic tone for not being au fait with the latest transpositions in the music world. "In that case, I'd better be going."

"Why not wait around? She should be here any minute to pick up the girls."

It was both good news and bad news. I was about to be united with a very dear friend from whom I had once been inseparable. At the same time I learned that the intervening years had not been kind to her. She was divorced and a single mother.

"No, I can't believe it." The voice was mezzo-soprano, the tone joyous, the timbre like a bell. It was Evie, looking at first glance no different than she had nearly twenty years ago. Brown hair cut short, her large hazel eyes shone as brightly as ever. Her cheeks were flushed from the windy March day, the surprise, or both.

Heedless of the onlookers, we rushed to embrace one another. Her perfume was the scent of spring flowers.

"Where the hell have you been for the last twenty years?" she demanded, continuing to hug me unself-consciously.

"It's a long story, Evie." I then modulated the subject. "I've just got to New York and I take it there have been one or two changes in your life."

"Yeah, you might say that," she acknowledged good-humoredly. "Come and meet the two most important ones."

She approached the pair of young girls, each wearing blue sweaters over white blouses. They were chatting to a Hispanic woman, who turned out to be a temporary nanny. It was unmistakable who they were. They looked like miniatures of their mother. They certainly had her charm.

Lily, thirteen, and Debbie, eleven, reacted with enthusiasm when Evie introduced me.

"This is my old friend, that genius pianist I've told you so much about."

"You mean the one that became a doctor instead?" asked Lily.

"And went to the jungle and never came back?" asked her sister.

"Almost right," their mother laughed.

"How did you hear I was in Africa?" I asked, my curiosity piqued.

"I have my ways," Evie answered playfully. "Actually, I've been keeping a lot closer tabs on you than you think. I have a secret source."

"What?"

"It's called the *Michigan Alumnus*. Your brother's been terrific about keeping the old grads up to date on your activities. Your family must be very proud."

Only then did she take a careful look at the left side of my forehead.

"It's barely visible," she said sympathetically. "I guess you were lucky, huh?"

"You might say that," I answered, intending it to sound ambiguous.

"What brings you to New York?"

I immediately realized that my fraternal chronicler had been a little less forthcoming about my more recent movements.

"Well, I suppose I'd have to say Cornell Medical School. I'm a professor there."

"Really?" she asked delightedly. "Has doctoring turned out to be everything you hoped for?"

"Do you want a simple yes or no answer—or can I take you and the girls for an early dinner somewhere?"

"Oh yes," her daughters cheered.

"Are you sure you haven't got anything more important planned?" Evie asked with a twinkle.

"Absolutely."

I then addressed the two girls. "Do you like the Russian Tea Room?" They both nodded eagerly.

Evie somehow caught her former husband's attention and exchanged waves that obviously signaled the transfer of authority for their children and we walked out.

Once we reached the street, the girls instinctively skipped ahead, which allowed me to say what was uppermost in my mind to their mother.

"Hey, I'm sorry the marriage didn't work out."

"I wouldn't quite put it that way, Matthew. We've got two wonderful girls and I wouldn't trade them for anything."

"But still, bringing them up on your own—you are on your own, aren't you?"

"This is New York," she answered. "The ratio is hardly what you would call favorable to single women."

She was in good spirits. I could sense that when we were alone I would hear the darker side of her breakup with Roger.

But for the moment we had reached the Russian Tea Room, and our attention would shift to *blinis* and sour cream and, of course, tea from the *samovar*.

It had been such a long time since we had seen each other that a great deal of basic information had to be exchanged. Not unexpectedly, she chose the girls as a high point and Roger's opting for the fiery Mexican as the low point. She spoke quite candidly in front of the kids, who had obviously lived through it blow-by-blow.

My own source of pride was the clinic in Eritrea, with the low point inevitably being the bullet. I glossed over it casually so as not to upset the girls. This left a whole further occasion to discuss Silvia—a topic definitely not suitable for children's ears.

Evie seemed as indomitable as ever. Even now, two decades after we first met, nothing altered my original impression of her. She was strong, resilient, optimistic, prepared to take the good with gratitude and the bad without self-pity as they chanced to come her way.

After the divorce she had obviously modified her career plans, but Roger had been generous enough to get her appointed at Juilliard, where she tutored privately, taught master classes in cello and still performed with various chamber groups at least in the Metropolitan Area.

Though I certainly had a valid excuse, I nonetheless felt irrationally guilty at having been absent from her life at a time of crisis when my friendship might have been of help to her.

"How do you spend your summers?" I asked, trying to confine our first discussion to neutral topics.

"Well, the girls join Roger and . . ."—you could see she still had trouble saying it—"Carmen for a month. Lately I've been going out to Aspen for the Music Festival. Now, why don't you tell me what you've been hiding?"

I was baffled. "What do you mean?"

"Her name, what she does, how many kids you have?"

"What are you talking about, Evie?"

"What do you think I'm talking about? Your wife."

"What wife?"

"The wife every halfway decent guy in New York always seems to have."

"I'm sorry to disappoint you, but I haven't got one."

She stopped and pondered for a second, obviously unsure of how to deal with what to her was a genuine anomaly. I knew what the next question would be and I sensed her struggling frantically to phrase it delicately.

"Oh, did it not work out?"

"Uh," I replied evasively, "I'll tell you about it another time."

"If it's not too painful for you."

"Oh, it isn't," I said unconvincingly. At least to Evie, who could still read my mind as well as ever.

At this point I turned my attention to the girls. I wanted to know them better and got the distinct impression that they had not enjoyed the afternoon with their father.

They were both cute—and as far as I could see, well-adjusted survivors of the nowadays all-too-frequent domestic shipwrecks. It was clear that their mother must have spent several difficult years taking care of them. For they were only now reaching the point where they could function without a parent every hour of the day. Good for Evie.

Dinner was over and the girls had polished off their Charlotte Russes. I hailed a cab and took them home. To my delight I discovered that they lived just down the block from me in the legendary Beauchamp Court.

"Your building is famous," I told the girls. "People have nicknamed it 'Carnegie Hall East.' They say it's the only apartment house in New York where every flat comes with a fridge, freezer, stove and Steinway."

"Yes," Debbie said. "Mom likes to call it 'philharmonic alley.'"

I looked at Evie and she smiled.

"That was one advantage of my getting sole custody. There was no pressure about who got the apartment. I not only enjoy living with so many musical neighbors," she gave a mischievous little smile, "I really like the fact that Carmen wanted it so badly and couldn't swing it."

"Oh, they still might," Lily piped up.

"What's this, honey?" Evie asked.

"It's kind of complicated, but Carmen said that if Mr. Sephardi gets the London job, his penthouse would be on sale and they'd be first in line."

I saw Evie react to the prospect with a loud but unspoken, "Shit." To comfort her I lied and said that I too might be interested in the apartment and would fight just as hard to get it. The girls seemed to like this idea a lot.

"Now tell me what I've been dying to hear," Evie said eagerly. "What are you doing musically at the moment?"

I groped for a reply.

"At the moment I'm going through all the Mozart piano concerti—"

"That's terrific," Evie exclaimed and then I added sheepishly, "only I'm letting Daniel Barenboim do the actual playing. I mean, I'm so busy in the lab that the best I can do is play the CDs over the sound system. But anyway, that's a long story and we can talk about it next time—which I hope will be soon."

In the elevator I could see Evie holding a wordless dialogue with her daughters and their signals of agreement to go ahead with what she was proposing.

"Uh, Matt, the girls and I would like to have you over for dinner."

"That would be great."

"What day would be best for you, Matt?"

"Well, I'm my own boss, so you guys choose."

We went through the complicated exercise of harmonizing

diaries. The girls had music lessons on Monday. Evie taught Tuesdays and Thursdays until ten-thirty. I had my seminars on Monday and Thursday afternoons. Then there were guest lectures at assorted times.

The first day we could clear was nearly a fortnight later, which I welcomed since I would need time to organize my thoughts.

Rediscovering Evie had opened up a vein of memories. Of missed opportunities, of chances lost. I should never have allowed us to drift apart.

One thing was sure. Now that we had found each other once again, our friendship would begin precisely where we had left off. And this time there would be no intermission.

# SEVENTEEN

THE TROUBLE WITH being an eccentric is that everybody notices when you act the slightest bit normal.

Thus two weeks later, when I left the lab at five-thirty, letting it be known that I would not be returning till the next day, tongues began to wag.

Actually, the damage had already been done in the morning, when I showed up with a decent hair-cut. There was no Medical Congress, no visitors from Washington, so why the hell should the boss want to look neat and presentable for no apparent reason?

I had even kept the details from my secretary, Paula. I had her mark the evening merely as "din-ner 7:30" with a note to herself to remind me to "take the dolls."

In my final days in Africa, I had cruised the nearby villages, in search of what I now knew were the finest craftsmen, acquiring—sometimes commissioning—figurines of the various different local characters, so that when I got nostalgic back home, I could look at them and remember who and what they were to me.

I looked at the population of my miniature Eritrea and tried to choose gifts for Evie's daughters.

At first I thought about bringing them tiny models of girls their own age. But in the end I selected the two that meant the most to me: a pair of old musicians playing native instruments—one a kind of drum, the other a long-necked fiddle. (They were exactly like the musicians at Aida's Christmas party.)

For reasons that I first could not comprehend, I decided not to give a doll to Evie. I guess I didn't want her to be part of what I left behind. And so I simply brought her flowers. I remembered that she loved narcissi.

"Carnegie Hall East" immediately lived up to its reputation. As I entered, I recognized a famous pianist and his wife obviously headed for a concert (not his own or he would have left much earlier). And the Italian elevator man chatted about music nonstop as he brought his clientele up to their destinations. Even to me, whom he immediately assumed to be a virtuoso of some sort.

Upon learning of my destination, he pronounced that Mrs. Josephson was "lovely lady. Excellent musician. But what is the most important: wonderful as mother." (Did he offer his considered judgments of the tenants to all visitors, or was Evie special?) He also noted, "My wife too is excellent as mother, though unfortunately she does not play instrument."

Unfortunately for him we finally arrived at Evie's floor.

It was no surprise to hear Rachmaninoff's Third Piano Concerto (live) emanating from her neighbor's apartment. But what struck me at that moment was the pungent aroma of tomatoes and garlic wafting from underneath Evie's door.

For some strange reason it made a deep impression on me. Of a real home dinner, not a restaurant or microwave. And waiting for me now to join them: a real family.

Debbie opened the front door, announcing that her mother had been held up at a faculty meeting, and had arrived home but minutes ago.

"Can you come back a little later?" she suggested helpfully. "We're not ready yet."

"Debbie," called Evie's disapproving voice, "bring Matthew to the kitchen this instant."

"Hello," she smiled when I entered. "As the head waitress just told you, I'm running slightly late. Would you mind opening the Chianti?"

While Lily grated the Parmesan cheese into a bowl, Evie poured the pasta into a colander. Her apron covered a simple but flattering dress, which I was sure she hadn't worn for teaching. The room was redolent with different smells. It was reminiscent of our student days long ago when we'd cook dinner and then stay up half the night making music.

We kissed each other on the cheek. I felt that Lily might not have liked such an overt gesture of affection, but I also sensed that Debbie would. And her blushing smile when I paternally patted her hair seemed to confirm it.

When the girls finished setting the kitchen table, I took out the presents, which they unwrapped with fascination. This fueled a conversation that took almost the entire dinner.

The memories of Adi Shuma I shared with them were just as vivid now as they had been six years ago because they lived inside me still: the endless lines of waiting patients who had stayed the night (and sometimes longer) just to see the doctor for what often turned out to be fleeting moments ("flying diagnoses," we had dubbed them.) The strange collection of unselfish characters who'd sacrificed the cushy jobs back home to help the victims of starvation, drought and civil war. The more profound experiences that permanently changed my attitude—like feeling guilty sitting at a meal like this.

They were impeccably behaved girls, who barely let their mother lift a finger either serving or to clear the table. Yet they patently ignored her unambiguous order to repair and do their homework. Evie had to spell it out as a command:

"I think you ladies better go and start your *devoirs,* or there'll be no time for telephoning."

With that threat they both decamped. Though a reluctant Debbie stretched out the time by petitioning her mother to allow her to return and "listen when you guys start playing."

"No one said anything about playing," Evie countered with a slight hint of embarrassment. "Matthew's had a long day and may just want to sit back and relax."

To emphasize the change of subject, she then turned to me and asked, "What time do you usually start at the hospital?"

A topic far more comfortable for me.

"Actually sometimes I spend whole nights at the lab."

This personality defect in me mistakenly impressed the girls.

"You mean you don't go to bed at all?" Lily asked wide-eyed.

"Oh, I always get a few winks curled up on my couch," I quickly explained.

"Is that why you're not married?" Debbie asked ingenuously.

Evie's face turned fire-engine red as she pulled rank.

"That's quite enough, young lady. You are now officially dismissed."

"Okay. See you guys later, I hope."

"Gosh, they're cute," I laughed and would have offered a much longer panegyric had not Evie's rubicundity subsided. "How can Roger bear to be without them?"

"Oh, he manages," she answered, her displeasure undisguised. "I think he even schedules his tours of the Far East to coincide with their vacations, so they couldn't possibly fly out and be with him—or rather them. As you may have gathered, Carmen is not exactly my favorite person. Believe it or not, she has three children of her own whom she religiously neglects. But, then, you know artistic temperaments."

"I'm sorry, Evie," I offered sympathetically. "That's not really fair to the girls or to you. I mean, *you* should have a chance to tour as well."

"Maybe when the girls are old enough. I'll just have to wait. Now you—we've heard about your medical exploits. Tell me what you're really doing musically."

I had come without illusions, knowing that the topic would inevitably be broached. After all, it used to be our bond, our common language. Could two fish possibly converse and never mention *water*?

Though I had pondered it, indeed spent many hours preoccupied with how I would present to her my (what could I call it?) lapse from music, I never hit upon words suitable to express it. And what could I offer her as a rational explanation? The trauma of the gunshot? That was plausible according to the psychoanalytic research I had consulted. But was this the case with me?

And besides, could I much longer avoid mentioning the spectral residue of my experience with Silvia? It made me what I was today.

Or perhaps more accurately, what I wasn't.

I had never revealed this to anyone. And only now, in opening my heart to her, did I begin to comprehend the full extent of the painful silence I had been living all these years.

I also realized as we talked that Evie was the only person in the world I could have shared this with.

I started with that afternoon in Crans.

"Oh God, Matt," she whispered sympathetically when she had heard it all. "It must have been devastating. How can you stand it?"

How many times had I asked myself that same question in the years that followed? How did I bear that first moment when I realized it was gone?

After a long silence, at last she offered:

"Beethoven. That's what it makes me think of. But even though he couldn't hear, he was still able to compose. He could create the *Ode to Joy* and hear it sung inside his head. You must feel mute."

"Please, Evie, don't exaggerate. I'm not a genius. The world's not poorer for my loss."

"But *you* are, Matt," she said, her voice so full of empathy it was as if she'd spoken through my mind.

We exchanged no words for a few minutes. Then she looked at me earnestly and said, "Tell me everything. Please, Matt, don't be afraid."

We talked late into the night. Of Silvia. Of Paris. Of Africa, and then her total disappearance.

Evie simply listened.

At last, when I had finished, she looked at me for a moment and observed, "You're still in love with her."

"I don't know. I guess she's still a presence in my psyche."

"All the time?"

"Of course not. Now and then. Like when I hear a piece of music that I played for her. Hey, look, it's not a big deal anymore."

"That's not how it sounds to me," she answered with concern. "But dammit, Matthew, why are you still pining after all this time? I mean, do you believe she ever thinks of you?"

"I don't know," I prevaricated. And then, "Unlikely." And finally, "Of course not. Not at all."

"You bet she doesn't," Evie said with anger. "For God's sake, music was the breath of life to you. How could you let her steal your very being?"

I had no answer for that and she still persisted.

"Come on, Matt. It's me, your old friend Evie. Look me in the eye and say that you can bear to live without your music."

How could I tell her that I couldn't? Or did she already see that?

She put her hand on mine and said this was the worst thing she could ever imagine happening to an artist.

I reminded her that I was a doctor.

"That doesn't make you any less an artist," she replied with feeling.

"Thanks." I whispered. "That means something when it comes from you."

She thought a moment and then asked, "Have you tried at all since then? I mean, even playing something simple, like the Minuet in G?"

"Evie, it's all gone. Every note. Even the silences within a phrase. I've more or less grown used to it. I mean, as a doctor I've saved lives. That was a kind of privilege. Believe me, if I had to choose . . ."

"But why should you, Matthew? Why should you be punished like this?"

In a way I now regretted having told her.

And yet in my heart I knew that had our paths not crossed again, I couldn't have survived much longer.

# EIGHTEEN

I BLAMED MYSELF for staying much too late. Evie would have to get up early and prepare the kids for school. I had no such obligations. Yet we'd been so caught up in talking we hadn't noticed the time.

When I got home I even had to fight off the ridiculous notion to call her as we used to in the old days, just to say thank you.

I was unwilling—or unable—to give in to sleep so I sat down and tried to dream up a casual pretext for another such encounter. (Perhaps inviting Evie and the girls to a concert or a matinee, a Sunday-morning bike ride through the Park, then brunch at Tavern on the Green.) As I mulled over the alternatives, I noticed that they all involved us as a pseudo-family. Why, in my catalogue of fantasies, had I not thought about inviting Evie out to dinner on her own?

Was I perhaps afraid of something like emotional involvement? But then, you idiot, what would you call the heart-to-heart communication you had with her tonight? You couldn't be much more involved than that.

I had an inner dialogue with Chaz, who asked sarcastically, "What's the problem *now*, big brother—scared of being happy?"

Answer: yes.

"But this is easy, Matt," Chaz lectured on. "She's been your friend for twenty years. This is not a new beginning; it's a natural continuation. Why don't you relax and let things develop?"

Sometimes my brother could make sense, especially in my imagination. And so I followed his advice.

I called the next morning and thanked Evie. She too sidestepped her own feelings, emphasizing that the girls had really liked me and had begged her to ask me again soon.

"Incidentally," she inquired, "are you interested in coming to Mozart's birthday party a week from Saturday? Every year a bunch of friends and colleagues get together in his honor. Everyone who wants to gets a chance to perform."

Uh-oh, sounded like a bit of pressure. But she quickly reassured me.

"Anyone who doesn't play an instrument can play the audience. So all you'd have to do is sit and listen and forgive the unforgivable mistakes."

"Mistakes?"

"Sure, they're a real mixed bag of musicians. My best pal, Georgie, teaches viola in our department at Juilliard. Her husband's an accountant and a real sweetie, but to put it mildly he's a keyboard klutz. We kind of close our ears because he's so enthusiastic. Would you like to come?"

"Sure, what will *you* be playing?"

"Well, I'm down for the quintets and whatever else they rope me into."

"Sounds like fun. What time should I pick you up?"

"Is eight o'clock okay?"

"That's fine. Should I bring anything?"

"Well, you can pick a nice white wine and I'll provide my famous lasagna."

"Great. I look forward to it."


LUIGI TRANSPORTED US TO THE PARTY—three floors down—at quarter speed, using the abbreviated journey to converse with me.

"The gentleman is a pianist, yes?"

"Who told you?" I reacted with a touch of paranoia.

Evie shrugged off all responsibility. Luigi then revealed, "Is obvious. You do not carry instrument. What could you play if not piano?"

"Well, I could sing," I joked.

Our interlocutor considered it for half a second and decided, "No, I do not think so."

Conversation ended. We'd arrived.

I was never very good at parties, which is why I was always so grateful for the chance of making music. On every possible occasion, except perhaps funerals, I was inevitably requested to perform.

Mind you, this time I was not at a loss for conversation, since the subject was familiar and I could hold my own discussing the new artists in the scene. What's more, I felt relieved to be "retired" when I met the music critic of the *New York Times*. The guy reviewed everything, including the hors d'oeuvres (lucky he liked Evie's lasagna or I would have belted him).

Good old Amadeus's repertory got a workout with much emphasis upon the strings. Then they reached the quintets, which are particular favorites of mine. The E-flat was the showplace for our host, the philharmonious accountant. Evie told me that he'd been practicing for this all year long.

While the other participants cheerfully took their places, tuning up and chatting, he stood anxiously and scanned the audience. For some unknown reason his glance fell on me.

"Hi, there," he smiled nervously. "Aren't you a friend of Evie's? I'm Harvey. I don't recall your name."

I introduced myself again. He was clearly in a state of panic about his moment in the sun.

"Uh, Matt, I've noticed you're not playing. But can you read a bit?"

"What did you have in mind?" I answered amicably.

"Would you be able to turn pages for me in this next one?"

"Sure, Harvey, I'd be happy to."

Evie was having an animated dialogue at the punch bowl, but our glances met. She smiled as if to say, "Enjoy yourself. I didn't plan this either."

Then we commenced, with Harvey laboring like Hercules just to keep up with the music. I felt like when I'd been an intern watching a particularly maladroit physician botching up a simple operation. This time I longed to intervene, and put Mozart out of his misery. And yet despite poor Harvey's fumbling it was nice being this close to the keyboard once again.

Thankfully it ended. And then Evie and some faculty friends

came up to play a string quintet. As she passed by she gave me a kiss and whispered, "You did a terrific job, Matt."

"Thanks," I laughed and kissed her back. I wasn't sure whether this simply was an excuse for some physicality, but in any case I'd made a friend in Harvey and had promised to turn pages for him if he should perform again that evening (please God, not).

True to her word, Evie did not allude to my past as a pianist. But it was quite evident she had confided in a friend or two about my future as a . . . partner? For almost everyone I spoke to gave an unsolicited endorsement of her as a person and as a musician. One man offered the opinion that her husband, Roger, "was a total schmuck to give up a gal like that. But sooner or later Carmen will add his gonads to her collection, and he'll come crawling back."

Not if I had anything to do with it.


WE STAYED SO LATE that Luigi had gone home. When we at last returned to Evie's, Bob the night man waited patiently to see if he should take me down. I wasn't sure what Evie wanted, but thank God *she* was.

"We haven't had much chance to talk this evening. Why not come in for a while?"

"Fine," I answered and Bob disappeared.

"I'll make some coffee, and we can have it in the studio," she suggested, pointing toward the room to the right of the front door. "Decaf or real?"

"Better make mine real. I'll be going to the lab later."

"At this hour?"

"It's kind of a tradition I've established. To make sure the guys that work 'the graveyard shift' on Saturdays get brownie points."

———

I WALKED INTO THE STUDIO and switched on the light. It was a real musician's paradise. Whatever wall space that wasn't lined with books was soundproofed in cork—should someone be inspired to perform at any time. The library seemed to contain every work that had been written on the cello.

Her music stand was set up by the window so she could gaze out at the river while she played. There also was a Steinway grand just sitting there.

Evie entered with a tray of coffee just as I had taken one step closer to the instrument. She had the infinite delicacy to say nothing.

I took the tray, set it down on a table, and put my arms around her.

We held each other tightly for a moment. Then we kissed, no longer merely as friends, now on the verge of being lovers. It felt completely natural. I disengaged myself from her after a moment and gently closed the door, so that the sound of our first lovemaking would stay inside the studio. The room for making music.

I WAS BORN AGAIN THAT NIGHT. I knew that I would wake and Evie would be there. Not just tomorrow or the next day, but an infinity of future mornings. I would now open my eyes, reach over and touch her. For the first time I felt an intimation of eternity.

In all the years I'd known her I had never even seen Evie in a bathing suit. So her body was a new discovery for me. I saw her breasts for the first time when I was kissing them.

Making love, Evie had displayed a tenderness and sensuality far beyond what I had dreamed she owned. How had I managed to suppress this longing I had always felt for her?

The rising sun seemed to welcome us as a part of nature's scheme of things.

I woke up in love.

AND THEN WE HAD TO SCRAMBLE. The girls were still sleeping, so there was time for us to make a semblance of propriety. Evie hurried to her room while I dressed quickly and straightened up the studio to look as if I had decided to "stay over" at the last minute. (I seriously doubted whether Lily and Debbie would buy that story, and yet I didn't think my presence would upset them either.)

In any case we all had breakfast as a family and when they went back to their rooms to do whatever girls do on Sunday mornings, Evie and I sat smiling at each other.

"Well, that happened rather fast," she laughed.

"I hardly think knowing each other for twenty years would put us in the hasty category. Don't you agree?"

Her expression said it all without the need for words. The only question was: now what?

We sat drinking coffee and pretending to browse through sections of the Sunday papers when we both were bursting to discuss our common future.

"Are you going home?" she asked.

"Eventually. I mean, sooner or later I've got to at least change my shirt."

"But after that?"

"I don't know. What do you have in mind?"

"Well, Matt, we started something. How do you propose we continue?"

"By doing precisely that, Evie, by continuing. The only problem is my apartment barely has enough room for your cello, much less your daughters."

"So why don't I invite you to stay here for, let's say, a week?"

"What about the girls?"

"Well, I agree there might be a problem there," she acknowledged, smiling. "I don't think they'd ever let you leave again."

And that's exactly what happened.

A WEEK BECAME A MONTH, then two, then three. One evening Debbie, never one to mince her words, inquired without a blush:

"Matthew, can I call you 'Daddy'?"

I looked at Evie as I replied. "That depends on whether your mother will let me call her 'Mrs. Hiller.'"

I had decided long ago, and was merely waiting for the right time to ask her.

"Well, Mom, are you going to say 'yes'?"

Evie was beaming. "Only if you and your sister will be bridesmaids."

"Does that mean we get to wear new dresses?" Lily suddenly popped out from wherever she was listening.

"Yes, my darling," Evie answered. "That will mean a whole new everything."

A WEEK LATER JUDGE SYDNEY BRICHTO made a housecall and united us as man and wife in the presence of Evie's daughters. Georgie the violist was Matron of Honor and my assistant, Dr. Morty Shulman, held the ring for me. As a special treat Georgie's husband, Harvey, played (what sounded like) the Wedding March.

All that remained was for us to inform our own parents. Mrs. Webster shouted congratulations in a voice so loud we could have heard it all the way from Iowa without the telephone.

Chaz went quietly berserk.

"Sorry, you've missed the ceremony. Hope you're not offended."

"That depends on whether I've also missed the party too."

"No, that'll be at Christmas when we visit you and Mom."

"Then I'm not offended. Congratulations, Matt, for proving that you're even smarter than I thought."

# NINETEEN

I WAS ALIVE for the first time. I only realized this after the first month of marriage. How could I have wasted so many years of utter incompleteness? Never really having lived with anyone, except for Africa, I had no idea what a marriage was like on a day-to-day basis. I wondered if someone as obsessively involved with his work as I could cut the mustard as a husband.

Yet by taking for granted that I could, Evie gave me the confidence to prove her right.

She also taught me how to be a parent. I was soon visiting the girls' school, talking over academic problems with their teachers just as if I had been doing so throughout their lives. (Roger's participation ended with his signature on each semester's check.) In a way, I had already learned so much in observing Evie (not to mention my experiences "raising" Chaz) that I had a head start on life's least user-friendly occupation.

IT WAS AS IF EVIE AND I had always been together. She instinctively knew how to live in the first person plural.

One of her favorite pastimes was visiting the all-night supermarket on the way home from a concert. It pleasantly extended the hours of our togetherness.

Indeed, on one of these nocturnal binges, Evie broached a brave new topic.

As she playfully flipped rolls of kitchen towels into our shopping cart, she commented out of the blue:

"Has it ever crossed your mind that I'm not too old to have another baby?"

"Why would you want to?" I replied ingenuously. "You've already got two great ones."

"Well, wouldn't it be nice if you and I tried one more as our own collaboration?"

I suddenly stopped tossing paper products and reflected. My own baby? One I helped to make myself? Having delivered lots of them I could, of course, recall the joy that the arrival of these little seven-pound people had brought their parents.

While she was waiting for my reaction, Evie casually dropped an ovulation kit into the basket.

"Wait a minute," I protested, putting it back on the shelf. "Can I have some time to think?"

"Sure, okay. It just was an idea."

I could tell she was disappointed. Yet my own experience at the receiving end of parenthood had not been such unadulterated bliss that I was certain I wanted to inflict it on another human being. Still, I would reconsider its potential with a person that I really loved.

"Let's wait a month or two," I said, feeling both slightly guilty and relieved, as we proceeded to the vegetables.

MEANWHILE, WE WERE BUSY BECOMING A FAMILY.

Sometimes I even enjoyed the "intergenerational warfare."

One night Lily announced a startling new development in her social life. Paul had arrived. She had met this "divine" Horace Mann junior at a party three Saturday nights ago and was now informing us in the most casual manner that she would be spending the weekend at his parents' country home in East Hampton.

"Well," Evie reacted, restraining what I am sure was inner apoplexy. "This is a little unexpected, Lily. Matt and I will need to discuss it. And naturally we'll have to speak to Mr. and Mrs. . . . ?"

"Hollander, but what difference does it make?"

"Because when I speak to the guy I have to know what name to call him," I replied.

"To whom are you referring?" she demanded.

"To Mr. Hollander, Paul's father."

"I'm sorry, Matthew, but I don't see why any of this should be your concern. Everyone important from my class is going and Mom's known them for years."

I looked at Evie. She gave me that special encoded look which meant, I know them and I don't like them.

"Listen, Lily," I reasoned. "I'm sorry I wasn't on the scene earlier to help supervise your growing up, but now that I am it's my responsibility to see that you're properly chaperoned."

"'Chaperoned!' My God, what century are you from? People don't have chaperones anymore."

"In that case," her mother interposed, imitating Lily's dismissive air, "you won't be going."

Her daughter had not expected this resistance and, of course, sought to ascribe blame.

"You put her up to this, Matthew, didn't you?"

"He did no such thing," Evie retorted.

"Then how come ever since he's been on the scene everything is so medievally strict? The man has no experience as a father."

"Stop calling him 'the man,'" Evie shouted, losing her temper. "And he's a better father than your biological one could ever dream of being. It's precisely because he wasn't around that I perhaps was a bit more liberal than I should have been. But you're not a little girl anymore."

"Oh, then you've noticed," she remarked facetiously. "Then there's no need to discuss this any further."

"Well, we finally found something we all agree upon," Evie concluded. "For the moment I suggest you go and do your math homework. Matt and I will discuss it and if we proceed to stage two, we'll call the Hollanders and find out what arrangements have been made for supervision."

"And embarrass me in front of all my friends?" Lily demanded.

"Not unless they're all listening on extension phones," I retorted. "In any case, if your mother and I are satisfied with—" I searched for a non-abrasive word.

"The policing aspect," our daughter proposed.

"If you wish to call it that. Then we'll see how it fits in with your schoolwork and come to a decision."

"And meanwhile, what am I supposed to tell Paul?"

"Tell him that if he is anything like the mature individual you've described, he'll understand our concerns and await our decision."

"No, I have to give him my answer tonight."

"*Pourquoi?*" asked I.

"Because that's when everyone else is telling him." With this she wafted out.

"After all, Evie," I explained with unfortunate jocularity, "we have to give Paul a chance to get another date in case Lily can't make it."

There was a sudden shriek from behind the door. It was not a voice I had previously heard in this house. But since Evie was stunned into silence, I concluded it must have come from the grown woman currently occupying Lily's room.

She stormed in again like a fury.

"Wait till my girlfriends hear about this," she warned us in a dire tone of voice. "Wait till they hear what kind of antediluvian parents I have."

"Hey," I said in genuine admiration. "'Antediluvian' is a really great word. Where did you learn it?"

"You, Matthew," she said, pointing her sorceress finger at me, "are nothing to me by blood or anything else. If you hadn't stopped sleeping in the lab we would all have been better off."

She marched off to inform her friends of my crimes against humanity.

Evie and I stood there looking at one another, unsure whether to laugh or cry.

In all, the maddening room-to-room guerrilla warfare lasted till nearly midnight, with Lily rearming herself by telephone between skirmishes. It was only after we solemnly promised "to give it serious thought" that she went to bed.

"What should we do?" Evie gestured helplessly.

"Well," I said, trying to keep my sense of perspective, "I wouldn't discuss having another kid right now."

THEN CAME THE WATERSHED.

The following summer I was invited to address the annual meeting of the International Neurological Society, this year being held in Rome. I wavered. Evie guessed the reason instantly.

"What are you afraid of, Matthew? Is Silvia beginning to assume mythical proportions in your mind?"

"Evie, I'm not afraid of meeting her, if that's what you're thinking."

"Then you're afraid of *not* meeting her."

"I'm not afraid of anything, dammit. Just let me tell you what I'd like to do."

"Okay, I'm listening," she said impatiently.

"Well, as I see it, Italy's not just a country. In the summer it's one great big music festival. There's a million different kinds of concerts: opera in the Baths of Caracalla, the arena in Verona, you name it. Why should I deprive you guys, and me, of this incredible experience? Let's spend at least a whole month there."

As she threw her arms around me, I let out a sudden growl.

"Aw, shit."

"What's the matter now?" she asked.

"Now I have to come up with a goddamn speech."

THE IDEAL TOPIC WAS OBVIOUS. For my keynote address, I would present the most up-to-date results of the procedure that had worked so well on Josh Lipton and, since then, half a dozen others.

Evie was terrific in helping me prepare. She even insisted that I go do a complete dress rehearsal in our room before delivering it to the vast throng of international nitpickers.

With its infinite gift for sensationalism, the Italian media picked up my research and I found myself being lionized by an excited swarm of reporters. I vaguely wondered if *La Mattina* was among them.

I also confess that, when the girls went out shopping on the Via Condotti, I went to the hotel operators' station and leafed through the Milan phone book.

Needless to say, her number was not listed.


I HAD PREPARED a special surprise for the girls. Evie's lifelong dream had been to visit Venice. So, I arranged for us to spend the entire last week there before we flew back home. Evie was deeply touched by the gesture.

The legendary city with the liquid streets exceeded all our expectations. We heard antiphonal choirs sing the sacred music of Giovanni Gabrieli in San Marco Cathedral, and that same evening Albinoni horn concerti performed under the magnificent ceiling by Titian in the Church of Santa Maria della Salute.

From the sublime to the ridiculous. The next afternoon, crossing the great piazza in a pastel sunset, we cringed as geriatric orchestras in neighboring cafés scratched out the corniest of pop tunes.

I suddenly realized that I was as happy as a man had any right to be. Impulsively I kissed the girls and hugged my loving wife.

The following day we visited the Gran Teatro La Fenice. This classic red-velvet jewel box of an opera house was the site of the original performance of *La Traviata,* my "first date" with Silvia. Now I stood for a long while behind the back row, gazing at the empty stage.

And somehow I felt the final curtain had at last descended. The heroine was no longer waiting in the wings, poised to appear when least expected in the theater of my memory. I would no longer be time's hostage. *Finita la commedia.*

A SEEMINGLY MUNDANE INCIDENT proved the turning point.

Evie was not a vain person. She cared little about her appearance beyond looking neat and appealing. Yet, when we were in the Hotel Danielli, I was surprised when I came out of the shower to see her looking at herself in the full-length mirror.

At first she didn't notice me and continued to crane her neck, trying to peek at her own back while pinching herself at the waist.

I knew exactly what she was thinking.

"You're fine, Evie. You have a lovely figure."

She blushed with embarrassment. "I didn't realize you were—"

She stopped herself and then spoke to the point. "You don't have to flatter me, Matthew. I know I've been overdoing it on the pasta."

"You haven't—"

"I've put on nearly five pounds."

"I never noticed," I said lovingly.

"Well *I* have. And I've got to do something about it before it turns you off. I'm going to get up early to jog tomorrow morning."

"Where do you expect to jog in Venice?"

"I'm told that at dawn San Marco's Square is like the reservoir in Central Park. Will you come with me?"

"Sure."

At six A.M. I hauled myself out of bed, quickly downed some black coffee and shuffled out to the piazza, where we joined at least a dozen motley—no doubt all American—fitness freaks, in outlandish garb and expensive footwear.

As I plodded along, I watched the look of determination on Evie's sweating face. She really loves me, I thought to myself. She wants to stay attractive in my eyes. She doesn't want to age. I guess she doesn't realize that one of her most endearing qualities is the fact that her beauty transcends time.

From that moment on I looked forward to growing old with my wife. I mean, I had already learned the difference between a *coup de foudre* that strikes a twenty-year-old and the profound love that captures a mature adult by slow and powerful osmosis.

This kind of emotion endures because it adapts to change. I could imagine Evie with gray hair, and I even knew she would care for me when I had lost all of mine.

Mature passion is not immutability, it is growth.

Suddenly I realized that in my imagination, Silvia, like the sculpted nymphs on Keats's Grecian urn, had never altered from the last moment I had seen her. In my daydreams she had remained forever young.

How could Evie's reality compete with Silvia's timeless perfection, unchanged and unchanging?

And then an odd thought occurred to me.

What if, despite the overwhelming odds against it, I had actually walked by Silvia at some point during this last month. How would I have known? I would have been looking for a tall, slender twenty-five-year-old beauty.

Yet now she had grown-up children. Perhaps her raven hair was now streaked with silver, her face slightly lined. Perhaps, like Evie, she had put on just a pound here and there.

My previous obsession had been fixed on a person who had disappeared. The Silvia I was remembering no longer existed.

I grabbed Evie's hand. She slowed down and stopped running.

"Hey, tiger," she smiled, herself slightly out of breath. "You'd better get your ass in shape."

"You're right," I grinned back. "Especially with a young wife like you."

Our arms around one another, we walked slowly back to the hotel as San Marco's Square filled with sunlight. And my heart with love.

# TWENTY

THE NEXT YEARS had the serenity of Beethoven's *Pastoral Symphony*. We were very happy. For a long time, anyway.

Then out of the blue came that damn phone call from Nico Rinaldi. Ironically, maddeningly, just when I thought I had finally exorcised her, Silvia reappeared in my life.

I should have said no right away. That would have been easier for all of us. Then it would have been over—quickly and painlessly. Like a bullet in the brain.

And yet a part of me could not help being curious. What was she like now? What had she become? And though it took a while for me to admit it to myself, something in me wanted to test the strength of my immunity to her.

———

I HAD TO SPEAK TO EVIE.

I knew her schedule by heart. At this very minute she would be in the midst of her Juilliard office hours. So I called her at once.

The moment I said hello, she sensed something in my voice.

"Matt, what's the matter?" She sounded concerned. "Is it the girls—?"

"They're fine," I reassured her.

"Are you all right?"

I began to tell her what had just happened.

Her reaction on first hearing Silvia's name was an involuntary "Oh." I quickly explained the reason for our imminent encounter.

Evie reflected for a second, then said quietly, "That's awful. Do you think you can help her?"

"Maybe, I don't know. But I feel kind of uneasy about it."

"Why? I mean, she's just another patient now, isn't she?"

I didn't answer instantly.

"*Isn't she,* for God's sake?"

"Of course." I tried to sound convincing.

"Then, what are you afraid of, Matt? You love *me,* you idiot. Look, it's going to be okay. You'll cure her. And then you'll finally *be* cured of her. Hang in there. I'll call you later."

She hung up. I could not help thinking, I wish I were as confident as Evie.


WHY DID I AGREE TO IT?

What could possibly be gained by seeing her?

Apologies? Some sort of spiritual retribution?

Or might it be—(I'm not above such feelings)—an unconscious

desire for revenge? For now our roles were diametrically reversed: Silvia was the wounded doctor, *I* possessor of the cure.

All this time I'd known that she was still alive because I'd read it in the papers. I'd come across the public messages announcing to the world that she was well, was married, had two children, had known familial joys. Did she ever once attempt to find out what became of me?

The violence of my growing anger took me by surprise. I never realized that I harbored such a resentment.

Just then the door to my office opened.

"Mr. and Mrs. Rinaldi," my secretary announced, superfluously.

Curiously, I looked at him first. I suppose I wanted to see what she'd preferred to me.

Tall, broad-shouldered, high forehead. We were both losing hair, but he more stylishly.

Nico wielded his charisma deftly. Firm handshake, voice secure and modulated. Completely in control.

"Doctor Hiller," looking me straight in the eye. "Thank you for seeing us so swiftly."

"Please sit down."

Did I betray the slightest hint of tremor in my voice?

At last I looked at her.

She was still very beautiful. The brilliance of those eyes had not diminished. When she entered any room she still illuminated it. Despite her illness and the passage of time, she seemed to have lost none of her magic.

She avoided my gaze even when she murmured, "It's good to see you again."

And then it became clear: she's afraid of me now.

Nevertheless, in this woman—exquisite even in the shadow of death—I recognized the person I had loved so passionately.

And like a man standing on the edge of the seashore, suddenly gripped by a powerful undertow, I felt myself losing balance.

They sat down side by side in front of my desk. Rinaldi held her hand.

Even after all this time, I could not help resenting his touching her. It was territorial, of course. He was reminding me that, although they were petitioning for my help, she belonged to him.

For her part, she sat passively, saying nothing. She still had difficulty looking at me.

Niccolo took the initiative. "Well, Doctor Hiller? I assume you've had a chance to read through my wife's notes?"

"Yes, Mr. Rinaldi. I have."

"And?"

"I'm sure I'm telling you nothing new when I say that the tumor is very advanced."

He seemed to take this as implicit criticism and felt obliged to defend himself.

"I was being cautious, Doctor. I thought the surgeon's knife was too great a risk. She's had the chemotherapy and radiation. In most cases that would have been sufficient."

Presumptuous idiot, I shouted inwardly at him. What qualifies you to judge what treatment she should have? Why didn't you bring her to me the moment they found the malignancy?

Merely to demonstrate that I had studied the folder well, I made a few general comments to them. Then, standard procedure required that I check the back of her eyes with an ophthalmoscope.

Needless to say, I had performed this routine a million times since the earliest days of my internship. Never before had I given any thought to the dimension of intimacy involved. But this was not an ordinary patient. This was Silvia.

"If you don't mind, Mrs. Rinaldi, I'd like to take a look."

She nodded.

I stood up, took my silver instrument and went toward her. As I came closer, I immediately recognized her perfume. It added a certain reality to what seemed a dream. I then bent over to look into her pupils. They were the same eyes I had gazed into as we made love, half a lifetime ago.

Inevitably our foreheads brushed. She was silent. I wondered if the same sensual memories were leaping to the surface of her skin. I remembered what it felt like to touch the rest of her. And I was surprised that I could feel so strongly after all this time.

I must have taken longer than I realized. My reverie was suddenly interrupted by the impatient voice of Niccolo Rinaldi.

"What is your opinion, Doctor?" he asked curtly.

I didn't answer him directly, but merely suspended my examination, stood up and retreated behind the ramparts of my desk. This was my last chance to escape, and I was determined to take it.

"Mr. and Mrs. Rinaldi, I've been giving this serious thought. I really think for everyone concerned it would be better if another doctor treated you."

"But you're . . ." he started to object.

"I don't mean by another method, since I do think the genetic route is all that is open to you now. But there are other experts doing this procedure equally as well as I. My colleague Dr. Chiu in San Diego—"

Silvia looked at Nico with helpless panic. She seemed about to say something to him, but he silenced her with a wave of his hand.

"I'll take care of this," he declared in Italian.

He stood up in what was perhaps an unconscious attempt to intimidate me.

"Now, Dr. Hiller," he began slowly. "Without going into detail, I can understand your reluctance to take on this case. I respect your feelings in the matter."

He then began to pace, as if appropriating my office as a podium.

"On the other hand, we all know that you pioneered this work. You've done it the most times and your record is the best."

He approached my desk, fixing my eyes with a saturnine gaze.

"Can you deny this to *Silvia*?" His right fist involuntarily hit my desk.

At this point she said in a frightened voice, "Nico, I think we'd better go."

He ignored her and remained determined to persuade me. But his tone this time was unmistakably a supplication. I could hear his voice almost choke as he said, "Please."

Clearly he loved her.

For the next few moments we all remained silent, thinking our own thoughts and wondering what I would do. At last I heard myself say, "Okay . . . okay, Mrs. Rinaldi." I took a deep breath and began, "I can't say I like what I see. There's considerable swelling of the optic nerve, indicating intracranial pressure, consistent with a tumor. But I don't have to tell you that, you're a doctor yourself. I know you've had it done already, but I'd like to take another MRI scan."

"Why, for God's sake?" Nico demanded.

I raised my head and gave him a stern glance that said in so many words, *Because* I'm *running the show*.

"I'll call the hospital and make arrangements. Is there a particularly convenient time?"

"No, we're at your disposal," he retreated into politeness.

"Thank you. Now, I must remind you that the tumor is dangerously large—even for genetic therapy."

"But you will try to treat it?" Nico interrupted.

I waited a split second before answering to make sure he understood I had given due consideration to his question.

"Yes, if there are no contraindications in the blood test. But none of us should cherish any false illusions."

I paused and then asked more gently, "Is that understood?"

Nico answered.

"Yes, Doctor. But assuming there are no, uh, problems, how soon could you begin?"

"I could have my nurse take some blood now to get the usual screens out of the way. That would mean, all being well, we can start as soon as we get the results.

"I would strongly advise you to remain in New York. With a malignant vascular glioma there's always the chance of hemorrhage. And the less moving around the better."

"There's no question," he agreed. "We have an apartment here and a full-time nurse, so my wife will be comfortable. As it happens, I have to fly to Italy in a few hours, but I'll be back the day after tomorrow at the latest. And I'm always reachable by phone."

"Fine," I said. And inwardly questioned how he could be so sublimely overconfident as to leave me alone with Silvia.


AFTER THEY LEFT, I sat there with my head in my hands, wondering why the hell I had ever agreed to see them.

I was tempted to cancel the rest of my patients. But then I did not want to be alone with my thoughts. And so, for the next few hours, I lost myself in the mortality of others.

At three o'clock the phone rang. It was Evie.

"How did it go?" she asked.

"All right. She's very sick."

"I'm sorry. But how did *you* feel?"

"Sad for her," I answered. Which was part of the truth, anyway.

"I can sense there's a lot to talk about. Why don't we meet at The Ginger Man and have a quiet dinner?"

"Good idea. I've got a seminar at four-thirty."

"Okay, fine. Debbie's got ballet and Lily has a violin lesson. By the time I round them up and give them their dinner, it'll be eight or so. You'll definitely be free by then."

"Absolutely. Unless Zimmerman starts one of his mega-orations. I'll call you when it's over."

She laughed. "See you later."

I hung up and tried to immerse myself in work, writing lecture notes and dictating reports. Since I had asked not to be disturbed, I ignored the phone ringing. After about fifteen minutes, my secretary buzzed me to say, "I know what you said, Matt, but Mrs. Rinaldi is very anxious to speak to you."

"Okay, put her through."

"Hello. Am I disturbing you?"

"That's all right, Silvia. What is it?"

"Can I see you? Can you come to the house?"

I was about to protest the fullness of my schedule when she pleaded, "I really need to talk to you."

I glanced at my watch. If I got Morty Shulman to take the seminar, I would have two hours and still could be on time for Evie. I proposed five o'clock and she accepted.

It was an unusually mild February afternoon. I needed to get some air and collect my thoughts, so I walked to their penthouse on Fifth Avenue and Sixty-eighth Street, wondering all the while what I was going to hear.

And whether I would be able to tell Evie about it afterward.

AN ITALIAN MAID in a black-and-white uniform answered the door, took my coat and accompanied me to the vast terrace overlooking Central Park. Silvia was reclining on a chaise longue, warmly dressed, her knees covered by a blanket.

She introduced me to Carla, her nurse, who had been sitting beside her. The woman rose respectfully. I explained that the blood-test results were fine and that I had scheduled the scan for the next morning at ten o'clock. At this point the nurse discreetly retreated.

I looked at Silvia and asked, "Why did you call?"

"When Nico left I suddenly got frightened."

"Of what, exactly?"

"Of dying." There was fear in her voice.

"But Silvia, I promised I'd do my best to help you."

She looked up at me. "I know that. And now that you're beside me I feel better . . . Matthew."

Her look, and especially the way she spoke my name, confirmed that I had not been wrong. Once, at least, however long ago, I had been the center of her life.

"Can you stay for a little while?"

I sat down next to her.

"I'm sorry that it has to be for this reason," she said quietly. "But I'm really happy to see you again."

I did not reply. I sensed the conversation was leading into areas off-limits to a doctor and a patient. But she persisted.

"Do you remember the end of your favorite Gluck opera—when Orpheus loses his beloved and sings that heartbreaking aria "What will I do without Eurydice"? That's exactly how I felt when I lost you."

Her analogy was the perfect description of what I had felt as well. But where was all this leading?

"There are so many things I have to tell you, Matthew."

It would be lying to say that I did not burn to know what had happened back then. That if I did not ask, I would go to my grave wondering how she could have loved me one minute and deserted me the next.

"Listen, I want you to know something," she said passionately.

I waited.

"You were the love of my life."

Though I had fantasized it at least a million times, I never really believed I would actually hear her say it. Her words took me by surprise, clouding my better judgment. Now I *had* to know.

"Then why, Silvia? Why did you marry him?"

She looked away.

"It's very difficult to explain. You'll never understand."

I could see she was distressed, so I chose my words carefully.

"Silvia, what exactly happened after I was shot?"

A sudden look of anguish crossed her face. The very thought of the incident seemed to cause her pain. She now seemed on the verge of tears.

"It was awful, Matt. Trying to get you back to the clinic alive was the worst nightmare of my entire life. I was sure you were going to die—and it was my fault. If only I had started driving when you first called to me. I've always blamed myself for what happened to you. My single memory of that whole journey is of you lying unconscious next to me and all I could do for you was stop the wound from bleeding. The next thing I knew, François and Gilles were lifting you out of the half-track.

"The moment you were safely in their care, the sky seemed to fall on my head. I just disintegrated." She covered her face with her hands and began to sob quietly.

I was touched by her account. I had never realized till this moment what a nightmare that long drive back must have been for her.

"I think I know what happened after that," I offered quietly.

She stopped crying and looked straight at me.

"François didn't have anyone capable of operating on the bullet. So you had to get me back to Europe. But the only way to bring me out of Eritrea was in one of Nico's helicopters from the Red Sea rig. And you called him, right?"

"Yes."

"And the price for saving my life was . . ."

She nodded guiltily.

"But that's blackmail. Jesus, if only you'd told me."

"Matthew, don't you see? I couldn't. I felt obligated. Especially since it did save your life."

I stared at her, scarcely able to credit that what I had always wanted to believe was in fact the truth. So, she had loved me after all. Her palpable sadness made me wish I could put my arms around her and comfort her.

And, in that instant I forgave her everything.

# TWENTY-ONE

WE SAT TOGETHER without talking, watching the sunset.

I was beginning to feel uncomfortable and anxious to break away.

And then Silvia sighed. "It won't be so bad now, Matt. If I die, at least I'll have seen you again."

"But you won't die, Silvia," I insisted. "I won't let you. I've told you."

She looked at me. "Somehow when you say that I believe it. How many people have you cured besides the Lipton boy?"

Ah, she had followed my career after all.

"Well, tomorrow I'll bring you a copy of my latest article in the *New England Journal*."

"No, I want to hear about them from you."

"Well, Josh is going to graduate high school next year. Katie just had a second baby. Donna Cohen and Paul Donovan are leading completely normal lives, and Sven Larsson's bowling team has just made the state quarter-finals."

"Is that all?"

"No, my technique has worked for teams in Denver and San Diego. But, you're a doctor too, Silvia. You know there's no such thing as a one-hundred-percent success rate."

I hoped she would probe no further and she did not.

Involuntarily, I glanced at my watch.

"Must you go now?" she asked forlornly. "Don't you even have time for a drink?"

"I'm sorry, I've got another appointment."

I remembered promising to call Evie after eight.

"Can't you put it off for a few minutes?"

She had already beckoned to the maid, who now stood awaiting her command. "Is it still white wine, Matthew?"

"Okay," I capitulated, annoyed with myself for giving in.

The servant reappeared quickly with a tray bearing a bottle of Puligny-Montrachet and two glasses.

Perhaps it was the glow of twilight, but there seemed to be a touch more color in Silvia's face. We gradually unlocked our memories and began to reminisce about the happy times. And these were many. Fifteen minutes became a half hour, and she then said, "You will have some dinner before you go?" This time I could easily have refused, but I stayed of my own volition.

We sat in the high-ceilinged dining room hung with canvasses by Renoir, Cézanne and Seurat, which made it look like an annex of the Jeu de Paume.

It was becoming increasingly difficult to restrict our conversations to the past.

"Did you ever see François again?" I asked.

"As a matter of fact, yes," she said. "In a way he sold out."

"What do you mean? He's got two thousand doctors working in thirty-five countries. How can you call that selling out?"

She looked at me and smiled.

"Nowadays he not only buttons his shirt, he actually wears a tie and jacket."

"Oh," I laughed. "That really is going bourgeois."

"We had dinner with him in Paris last year," she continued. "He was trying to charm a contribution out of Nico. By the end of the evening we were a few million dollars poorer and he had a field hospital in Gabon."

"Speaking of hospitals, what did you end up specializing in?"

She responded with a hint of a frown. "I had to give up medicine a long time ago. But that's another story."

"Tell me," I said. "I'm curious to know what could possibly have dampened your incredible idealism. I mean, you were so wonderful with children. I'll never forget that sub-acute you diagnosed on our first afternoon in Eritrea."

"Well, Matthew, that was Africa. Italy is quite another matter."

"Meaning?"

"Medicine and marriage don't mix so easily. It wasn't like my mother running *La Mattina* from a corner of the house. I don't have to tell you how demanding pediatrics is. Besides, Nico needed me around in the evenings, and the children of course."

I began to wonder if this was the same Silvia I once knew. I had difficulty hiding my disappointment.

And she sensed it.

"I am sorry, Matthew, but you always expected too much of me.

You cannot make Mother Teresa out of a spoiled Milanese girl who always got her own way."

"Come on, Silvia. I know who you were. It's *you* who've forgotten."

"All right, Doctor," she said, throwing up her hands. "Cherish your illusions."

"Anyway, I'm still involved," she said a trifle apologetically. "I'm a trustee of the hospital. And next year I'll be president of the Italian Red Cross."

My pager suddenly bleeped. I pulled it out. The liquid crystal display read: CALL YOUR WIFE 555-1200.

I quickly excused myself and dialed the number.

"Are you all right?" Evie asked. "Where are you?"

"There was an emergency," I replied evasively. (I'd explain everything to her when I got home.) "I'm on my way now."

"Come as soon as you can. We've got a lot to talk about. I'll have something ready when you get back."

"That's okay, I grabbed a bite. I just want to see you."

"I'll be waiting, Matt."

I then turned to Silvia.

"I'm afraid I've got to hurry."

"Of course, I understand. I've kept you too long as it is. Will you play the piano for me tomorrow?"

I felt a sudden chill.

"I'm sorry, Silvia," I said impatiently. "I've really got to go."

As we went to the door, she took my arm.

"You can't imagine how wonderful this evening was. Thank you for everything."

I walked slowly home, full of thoughts.

———

"YOU ARE ARRIVING LATE," our elevator man declared. "An emergency?"

"Yes, Luigi, an emergency."

"Is difficult sometimes to be a doctor, yes?"

"Yes," I answered, in a tone that I hoped would discourage further dialogue.

Unfortunately, I was one of his favorite conversation partners and he always drove at half speed.

"Mrs. Hiller is still awake," he informed me.

"How do you know?"

"I hear her practicing."

That at least was a valuable piece of intelligence. For when it came to practice, Evie was a day person. The only reason she played at night, unless it was for a concert, was to let off steam.

And who the hell could blame her for being pissed off?

It was nearly eleven o'clock. She was still making music when I entered the apartment.

"I'm home," I called as I walked in and headed for the studio.

The piano accompaniment for Franck's Sonata in A was booming from the giant Bose speakers—but then she was also playing much too loudly. I didn't know if she heard me enter, but she was not startled when I kissed her on the back of the neck.

"How was it?" she asked, still rapt in the music.

"It's been quite a day," I answered. "Want something to drink?"

"Yes," she replied. "Whatever you're having."

I returned with a glass of California Chardonnay for each of us. But she did not leave her instrument. It was then that I realized that she wanted the cello as a third-party witness to our conversation. At last she put her bow down and took a sip.

She waited for a moment and then said with studied casualness, "Was she still beautiful?"

I tried not to look at her as I admitted, "Yes."

She hesitated for a moment and then asked, "Are you still in love with her?"

"No," I said quickly. Perhaps too quickly.

She picked up the bow and began to play again.

"What did you talk about?"

"The past."

"Anything in particular?"

"I was right—Nico did force her to marry him."

"Lucky for me," she said, not smiling.

She then played a long passage of music without speaking. I sensed she was preparing something important to ask me. I was right.

"Is there anything you want to tell me?"

I thought for a moment and then worked up the courage to say, "Yes. I spent the evening with her."

She could not disguise the hurt my admission had caused her. Why the hell didn't I tell her on the phone?

"I'm tired," she said. "I'd like to go to bed."

FIVE MINUTES LATER, she turned off her light and lay back on the pillow. I thought momentarily about putting my arms around her and perhaps initiating something physical. As I hesitated she turned over with her back to me. I murmured, "I love you, Evie," but she seemed to have lapsed quickly into slumber.

I closed my eyes but could not sleep. At last I put on my bathrobe and went into the living room to look out the window at the sleeping city.

And wondered where it all would lead.

# TWENTY-TWO

AT TEN FORTY-FIVE Silvia's driver called to inform us that they were two blocks from the hospital. I dispatched Paula to meet them at the entrance.

To hear her tell it later, the limo was as big as a Boeing 747. When they both arrived at my department, every head turned. Silvia was by far the most glamorous patient I had ever treated.

Even though time was of the essence and we were all ready to go, she insisted on making the rounds of the lab to see the various pieces of futuristic apparatus that we used for restructuring DNA. And, most important, to meet the people working them, as if by charming everyone she could somehow influence the outcome.

I introduced her first to my assistant, Dr. Morton Shulman, lavishly praising his scientific acumen. Should I ever be unavailable, I wanted her to be completely confident she would have a clued-in doctor in my place.

Resa drew Silvia's blood and I showed her the machine that would "launder" it.

Mort and I then accompanied her to Radiology on the tenth floor, and stayed with her as she was strapped into the huge MRI machine.

When the session was over I asked Morty to take her down for coffee, while I hastened backstage to discuss the new photographs with Al Redding. As we walked to the elevator, I said to Silvia, "Dr. Shulman is a tremendous raconteur. Make sure he tells you about his Rollerblading mother-in-law."

By the time I got back, the senior radiologist and his assistants had the pictures on the viewing box and were studying them closely.

"You don't see many like this, Matt," Al greeted me gravely. "It's a real bitch. Have a look for yourself."

The damage was visible from halfway across the room: a splotch so large that it first seemed like a defect on the film.

"How can she still walk around with something that big?"

"She won't for long," the somber radiologist remarked.

"That woman will be dead in less than a month."

One of the residents then turned to me and asked respectfully, "Dr. Hiller, what are the chances of your therapy working with a patient that advanced?"

I was in no mood to share my thoughts with anyone else and so I simply answered:

"I'd like to study it alone for a few minutes. Is that okay, Al?"

"Go ahead," he agreed. "The boys and I will go down and grab some lunch."

They left me in the room with the image of Silvia's brain ravaged by that growth that, barring some unforeseen miracle, would certainly kill her.

The full reality of it suddenly sank in. This was Silvia, my first love.

My God, I thought to myself. She's still young. She's barely lived out half her life. And now she'll never see her children married or play with her grandchildren.

Or was there still a chance my protocol could save her?

My mind was far too clouded by my feelings. I needed an objective view of someone I respected in the field.

The timing worked out perfectly. It was noon in New York, which meant nine A.M. on the West Coast. And I caught Jimmy Chiu in San Diego just as he was about to start his rounds.

I greeted him laconically and requested that he do me the favor of reading the MRI scan, which I was about to transmit to his hospital's teleradiology computer.

Jimmy was a friend. He sensed my urgency and said he'd go right upstairs and look at it. Since the technician in New York was at lunch, I scanned the film into the machine myself, which sped a digitized facsimile of Sylvia's brain to San Diego, where it would reappear on the monitor in Jimmy's hospital.

HE WAS ON THE PHONE TO ME in minutes.

"I just want to know what you think, Jim. Could a patient with that tumor still be treated by the retrovirus route?"

"Are you serious? That glioma's so damned large, if it doesn't kill her, it'll cause a hemorrhage that will."

"Not even worth a try, huh?" I still would not give up. He could sense that I was hoping he might reevaluate his judgment.

"Come on, Matt, there are limits. We should concentrate on lives that can be saved. By the way, can you tell me who it is?"

"Sorry," I answered. "Thanks for your help, Jim."

I hung up quickly. With no need to act the stoic professional for anyone, I buried my head in my sleeve and cried. *Silvia is going to die, and there's nothing I can do about it.* Then gradually I remembered that at this very moment she was waiting for me downstairs.

I hurried to the men's room, washed up and made myself presentable again.

Ironically I found her laughing. Morty Shulman was regaling her with his best stories.

She noticed me approach and brightened further, waving me to join them.

"You two doctors really should be on the stage," she smiled. "I mean, Matt could be a concert pianist and Morty have his own television show."

My younger colleague looked at me with surprise.

"Hey, I didn't know you played."

"At about the level of your humor," I volleyed back, brushing off the question.

I sat down and looked at Silvia more carefully than I had ever looked before. Now for the first time I could see a shadow of impending death on her face, and I suspected that she knew it too. Her radiance today was just a kind of final blossoming before the flower died.

But either out of denial or sheer willfulness, she kept on talking about her future plans. From the productions they were planning for next season at La Scala to the trips that she would take that summer with her children. All things no longer possible.

MORTY AND I BOTH SAW SILVIA to her car.

"Jesus, Matt. Have you ever seen a bigger limo?" he remarked as they drove off.

"I've never seen a bigger tumor either, Mort. She hasn't got a prayer."

"No," he was genuinely shocked. "Not that wonderful, vibrant woman."

"Now, Mort," I tried to interrupt him, "I'm going to ask you for a special favor."

"Shit," he continued with dismay. "I can't believe it."

"Shut up and listen," I commanded him. "From now on Silvia's your patient. You'll take care of her and see to it that she doesn't suffer for a second. Do you hear me?"

The assignment clearly caused him pain.

"But Matt, she came all this way to be treated by you—"

"Just do it, Mort," I ordered.

"Okay," he nodded with reluctance.

"Good, now go up to Paula and take over my whole schedule till further notice. Both of you make sure that Resa gets whatever help she needs to prep the infusion for Silvia as fast as possible."

Morty must have thought I'd lost control of all my senses.

"Did I hear you right? One minute you tell me it's hopeless, and the next you want us to accelerate the whole damned procedure? I mean, the guys are overstretched already. Can you tell me why?"

"Because, you stolid scientist," I reacted furiously, "there still might be a miracle."

# TWENTY-THREE

I HAD GIVEN SILVIA strict orders to take a nap when she got home, as the morning activities would have taken their toll.

So for the next two hours I sat in my office, trying to prepare myself for her inevitable questions about the scan. I'd keep the truth from her, of course, but then I've never been very adept at lying. I only hoped the fact that we were going forward with the treatment would give some credibility to my prevarication.

Eventually I phoned her, and she urged me to come over as soon as possible because, as she explained teasingly, "I've got a special surprise for you."

Ten minutes later I was at her front door.

She took my hand as I entered the apartment and led me to the terrace, where an elaborate tea had been prepared.

"Sit down, Matthew. You won't believe what fate has brought us."

It was not so easy to maintain my equanimity, especially since I was now so much more aware of how fragile she really was.

"You'll never guess what's at the Met tonight."

"I don't know," I joked. "The Three Tenors?"

"No, Matthew, be serious. What was 'our' opera? *Traviata*, of course. And tonight Gheorghiu and Alagna are singing. As you know, they're lovers in real life."

"I suppose you've got a box there too?"

She laughed. "By chance, we do. As my doctor, would you allow me to go, and will you join me?"

"Yes, on both accounts," I answered, inwardly rejoicing that there still was something that could bring her such happiness.

"When is Nico coming back?" I asked.

"Tomorrow morning," she replied without enthusiasm. "He called just after I got back from the hospital."

"Sounds like an attentive husband."

"Yes," she said vaguely. "I do believe he loves me very much."

"How about your children? I know you have two boys. I mean, your lives are so public. Where are they at school?"

"In England, at Eton. Nothing's really changed. We're more paranoid than ever about their safety. Nico has them guarded around the clock. But it's all hi-tech now, and they don't seem to mind as long as it doesn't get in the way of their social lives. I hope you meet them someday. They're as different as chalk and cheese. The older one, Gian Battista, is the portrait of his father, and there's not a single sport he doesn't excel at. As far as I'm aware, he's never opened a book in his entire life. And yet, just like Nico, he can be irresistible. Naturally he was my father's favorite. I think the future of the FAMA dynasty is secure."

"He must have died a happy man."

"Yes, that's what he wanted. And then there's my little Daniele, so shy and bookish."

"He'll be the doctor, huh?" I suggested.

"No, I don't think so. He's too sensitive a soul. He'll be the poet, which is something of a first for both our families. He's so compassionate and caring. He's always marching for the underdogs in Bosnia and Rwanda."

I could tell she had a soft spot for her younger son.

"I think in another age he might have become a priest."

"How old is he?" I asked.

"He'll be sixteen in February."

I felt an ache because I knew she wouldn't be there.

"How many children do you have?" she asked.

"My wife has two daughters from her first marriage. I'm very fond of them."

"Yes, I can imagine you would be a lovely father, especially for girls. What's she like?"

"Who?"

"Your wife."

I didn't know where to begin or whether I wanted to. I simply answered, "She's a cellist."

"Oh," said Silvia. "That must be convenient."

"What do you mean?"

"I mean the two of you must play duets."

I suddenly felt my privacy being invaded and didn't want to answer at all. The wisest thing seemed simply to say yes and change the subject.

She then excused herself to dress for the evening.

"You surely must have calls to make—your other patients and the lab."

"Yes," I reacted with appropriate professionalism. "I'll check with the lab and see how things are going."

Left alone I dialed a single number.

"Yes?"

"Hello, Evie."

"Where have you been? You're not replying to your pager."

The truth is I had deliberately shut it off along with everything that was not Silvia.

"Sorry, it slipped my mind. Listen, about tonight."

"Have you forgotten it's Thursday, Matt?" she chided. "I've got a master class. I won't be home before ten-thirty at the earliest. Anyway, I'm rushing to pick up Debbie. Was there anything special?"

"No, I just wanted to hear your voice."

"Well, you're hearing it say goodbye. See you later."


SILVIA REAPPEARED, LOOKING ELEGANT.

"It's definitely going to be a repeat of Paris," I allowed. "I'm underdressed again."

"Don't be silly. Come on, we'll be late."

We went downstairs. Her car was waiting and we drove off toward Lincoln Center. Only then did I become aware of what a risk I was about to take. The Opera House was barely a hundred yards away from Juilliard. If there was any spot in the entire city where the odds of running into Evie were highest, it was there.

And as if by prearrangement, when we stopped for a traffic light on Broadway, I looked out the window and saw her standing on the corner of Sixty-fifth Street, carrying her cello. "Goddamn," I muttered under my breath.

Silvia immediately sensed what was happening. "Don't worry, Matthew, you can't see through these windows from outside." Then she turned and looked again, remarking, "The cello's almost as big as she is. Oh, and she's very attractive."

I said nothing as I stared at Evie's face.

I had always thought that the exquisite Silvia outshined my wife, whose true beauty was inward. And yet, ironically, this evening Evie looked lovelier than ever. Perhaps it was the aura of sadness in her soft hazel eyes. I felt a strong compulsion to leap out of the car and take her into my arms. Oh, Evie, I'm so sorry that I've hurt you.

LOVERS PLAYING LOVERS.

It was perhaps the most memorable performance of *Traviata* ever given, yet I was scarcely moved. The opera had lost its magic for me. I no longer sympathized with Alfredo's infatuation or believed Violetta's sacrifice. I sat there impassively until she sang her final aria. Now the part that had brought us both to tears in Paris so long ago had acquired a new personal dimension: "Oh Lord, to die so young . . . so close to finding happiness."

I looked at Silvia and noticed she was not crying.

On the contrary, her face had a strange look of serenity. She took my hand, the only time that evening, and whispered, "I've been close to happiness as well."

---

HALF AN HOUR LATER WE DREW UP in front of her house.

"This was a wonderful evening, Matthew. Will you come up for a drink?"

"No, Silvia. I can't."

"Please. Nico's away, it's my nurse's day off. I just can't face being on my own."

Knowing what I now knew, I could not refuse.

"All right. Just for a minute."

Upstairs it became clear that this had not been a sudden whim on her part. An elaborate supper for two had been laid out in her dining room. I was beginning to feel manipulated.

The maid immediately poured the champagne, which I drank perhaps a little too quickly.

As the meal progressed (I noticed she barely ate anything), she suddenly leaned toward me and said with emotion:

"Matthew, there's something I want you to know. Whatever happens, I'm leaving Nico. I've come to realize that life is too precious to waste on idle fantasies. And if you'll have me, I want to be with you."

*Please, Silvia, don't go on.* I tried to extricate myself as gently as I could and said with quiet finality, "I'm sorry. It's too late—for both of us. You can't make eighteen years of marriage just disappear. And I have someone in my life who's very precious to me."

"Matthew, don't I mean anything to you anymore?"

"Silvia, you are and always will be a beautiful memory."

I stood up.

"I really have to go now."

"No, please don't—" Her eyes filled with tears.

Foolishly I stopped and she drew nearer.

"You can't deny me this." She threw her arms around my neck and pulled me toward her.

Just then the door opened and Nico entered.

For a moment we were all paralyzed.

"Good evening," he said, clearly restraining his fury. "I'm sorry my early arrival has disturbed you." And then pointedly, "Good night, Doctor."

"No," Silvia angrily objected.

Nico turned and overruled her. "*Yes.*"

"I was leaving anyway," I said. "Good night."

Still in shock, I rang for the elevator. A split second later from inside the apartment, I heard Silvia shout, "Nico, you don't understand. . . ."

And then a sudden muffled sound like something falling.

The next moment their front door opened and Nico, ashenfaced, called out to me, "Doctor, come quickly."

I raced back inside. Silvia lay on the floor, motionless. I could see instantly what had happened.

I bent down to examine her further and ordered Nico, "Call an ambulance—quickly."

As I heard him on the phone frantically summoning medical assistance, I looked at Silvia, and saw for the first time a face that was not only beautiful, but finally at peace.

I would always remember her like this.

# TWENTY-FOUR

TWENTY MINUTES LATER we arrived at the Emergency entrance of the hospital. Mort Shulman was waiting. They immediately rushed Silvia to intensive care. But until the patient is hooked up to the life-support machines, the closest relatives—even if they are Nico Rinaldi—are not permitted to go in.

I could have, but chose instead to wait outside with him. He looked at me, confused.

"Shouldn't you be in there?"

"She's Dr. Shulman's patient now."

"As of when?"

"This morning. I'm staying here to keep you company."

If anything, this threw him even more off balance.

"What the hell's happened?"

"A hemorrhage, most likely. It was always a

possibility, and I'm afraid the tumor had grown considerably since her last scan."

Suddenly he was silent and a look of immense sorrow had taken over his face.

"I'm sorry, Nico. I know this will be hard for you to hear, but it would be merciful if she didn't wake."

He covered his face with one hand, shook his head from side to side and began to moan, "You're wrong, you're wrong. She has to live."

He stopped speaking, clearly trying not to let himself break down. I tried to comfort him.

"Nico, if there's any consolation, there was nothing you or anyone could possibly have done to change the outcome."

"No," he objected adamantly. "It's my fault. I should have brought her to you earlier, but I kept her away because . . . It's so difficult to explain. I loved her so much. I've loved her ever since she was a little girl."

I felt so sorry for him.

Suddenly he looked at me.

"I'm sixteen years older than her, Matthew. I should have been the one to go first. That's nature's way, isn't it?"

He stood rooted to the spot. Just then a nurse appeared to inquire if she could bring us anything. He waved her away. I asked for two cups of coffee.

Instinctively I took Nico's arm and led him toward a bank of plastic chairs. He had suddenly become docile and even seemed to have grown smaller. I sat him down. He began to weep quietly.

We remained without speaking for a long time. Then out of the blue, he turned to me and said without rancor:

"You didn't really know her. Deep down she was a child, a frightened child. How could it be otherwise after what happened to her mother . . . ?"

I listened, wondering where this was leading.

"When you were attacked in Africa—when you were shot, she was terrified."

What was he driving at?

"She begged me to protect her, to marry her right away."

What was the point of arguing this now? What did it matter? I just let him talk. It was something that he wanted me to know, and so I listened.

"I always knew she was a creature of expediency. To her mind, at this moment you were the stronger. You held the possibility of life in your hands. Silvia's first concern was always her own survival. That's what brought her to me twenty years ago and to you today."

I looked at him for a moment and then said gently, "Nico, what purpose is there in my knowing this? How does it change anything?"

"Because it's important to me that you understand. She was mine in life and she is mine in death."

Just then Mort Shulman appeared. He was ill at ease, clearly unaccustomed to the role he was now about to play.

"Mr. Rinaldi," he said barely audibly. "I'm sorry . . ."

Nico lowered his head and crossed himself. "May I see her, please?"

"Yes, of course."

Mort began to lead him toward the room, then suddenly the grieving husband stopped and turned to me.

"She was extraordinary, wasn't she?"

Without waiting for my reply, he turned again and walked away.

Yes, Nico. She really was.

# EPILOGUE

IT BEGAN TO RAIN. I turned my collar up and let the shower soak me to the quick.

I went down to the East River and began to walk aimlessly. Hardy joggers passed me by in both directions, savoring their masochism. I kept walking. My heart ached.

After almost two hours it gradually occurred to me: For the first time in nearly twenty years I was free, completely free. The ghosts that haunted me had disappeared.

Darkness had fallen and I suddenly became aware that my pager was bleeping. I reached into my pocket and pulled it out.

The screen displayed a short message: YOUR WIFE IS WAITING.

AT LONG LAST, wet and shivering, I put my key in the lock of our front door. I stepped inside and heard the sounds of the Brahms F Major Sonata. It was my beloved wife, embracing her cello, completely engrossed in the music while staring out of the window, her back to me.

As usual the piano accompaniment was coming from a loud-speaker. Evie's concentration was so intense that she did not notice my presence. It was only when I shut the hi-fi off that she realized I was there. She looked up. Before she could speak, I raised my finger to my lips to silence her.

She watched me wordlessly as I went to the shelf and found the piano copy of the Brahms.

I sat down at the keyboard, put the light on and began to turn the pages till I got to where she'd reached. I then turned to her and said softly, "Shall we take it from number one nine four?"

She nodded incredulously.

Slowly, tentatively, I began to play to her.

It was not easy and my fingers were not nimble. But, however awkwardly, I still was playing. Alone I introduced the second theme. Evie raised her bow and answered me by repeating what I'd played. We then joined together and conveyed our feelings to each other in the language of Johannes Brahms.

Miraculously and yet, at the same time, the most natural of acts—we were reunited musically. And as we played I tried to com-prehend what had suddenly allowed me to break out from the prison of my muteness. Had let me talk again. Had let me *sing*.

We paused at the great F-major chord.

"Evie . . ." I began.

She cut me off.

"Let's play the second movement."

She started the slow *pizzicato,* and then continued with long weeping notes, over which my piano part hovered, embracing her melody.

For a few moments the only sounds in the entire world were the harmonies of our relationship.

"I've always loved you, Evie," I said quietly. "I mean, always. From the very moment we met in school. I was too shy to put it into words. I tried to tell you sometimes when we played."

"Yes, I know," she said, tears streaming down her cheeks. "If only you had heard me answer you, you never would have let me go."

"But does it make any difference now?" I asked.

"No, Matt," she whispered. "We're together and that's all that matters."

The next movement was *allegro passionato.*